LOVE UNDER TWO HONCHOS

Lusty, Texas 3

Cara Covington

MENAGE EVERLASTING

Siren Publishing, Inc.
www.SirenPublishing.com

A SIREN PUBLISHING BOOK
IMPRINT: Ménage Everlasting

LOVE UNDER TWO HONCHOS
Copyright © 2011 by Cara Covington

ISBN-10: 1-61034-417-0
ISBN-13: 978-1-61034-417-3

First Printing: March 2011

Cover design by *Les Byerley*
All art and logo copyright © 2011 by Siren Publishing, Inc.

ALL RIGHTS RESERVED: This literary work may not be reproduced or transmitted in any form or by any means, including electronic or photographic reproduction, in whole or in part, without express written permission.

All characters and events in this book are fictitious. Any resemblance to actual persons living or dead is strictly coincidental.

Printed in the U.S.A.

PUBLISHER
Siren Publishing, Inc.
www.SirenPublishing.com

LOVE UNDER TWO HONCHOS

Lusty, Texas 3

CARA COVINGTON
Copyright © 2011

Chapter 1

Joshua Benedict wanted to scream.

He tried to be discreet when he checked the time on his Rolex Daytona watch. His brow furrowed as he calculated the time it would take for them to drive from Lusty to Houston, park in the underground lot, take the elevator up to their penthouse, check their messages, shower and change and head out for their date with luscious Lola.

Josh made a note to stop thinking of the lady in question as *luscious Lola*, because sure as hell that moniker would slip past his lips. He and his brother Alex were going to do their level best to show Lola Dell, accountant, that they respected her brain, her feminine integrity, and that they considered her to have value as a worthwhile member of society, and that she was, in every way, their complete equal.

Although he would admit, under duress, that he really didn't understand women very well, he did know one thing. If she thought for one moment that it was her G-cup bra that had been the first thing to draw them to her, and the main reason they had put her on their list in the first place, they would be toast.

He shot a glance to his brother, Alex, and noted his closest sibling seemed equally concerned about being late for their date, too.

The quarterly meeting of the Lusty, Texas Town Trust usually only ran for two hours, tops. This one was already twelve point eight percent over that median. Of course, there'd been the official introduction of the soon-to-be members of the family—Josh and Alex's future brothers-in-law Colt Evans and Ryder Magee.

That had been an important item on the agenda, and now that their sister was officially engaged, Josh supposed it would be appropriate for him and Alex to boast about being the ones to get them together in the first place. Even if their reasoning in doing so had been less than laudable, and the end result the complete opposite of what they'd been aiming for.

"Well, I think that's about it," Caleb Benedict, one of Josh's fathers and today's meeting chairman, said. "If there's nothing else?"

Before Josh could jump to his feet and make a mad dash for the interstate, the door to the Trust's boardroom—fittingly in the back of the Lusty, Texas Heritage Museum—burst open.

The woman who stood there wouldn't measure up to Josh's shoulder. She was tiny, white-haired, and had not that long ago celebrated her ninetieth birthday. One sight of her, and Joshua knew with absolute certainty that he and Alex weren't going to be racing off to luscious Lola tonight. Under the circumstances, that was fine with him. The lady drawing everyone's surprised attention at the moment was the only one he'd willingly miss a chance at those G-cups for. A big grin split his face. He figured the other members of his family were just as surprised—and as pleased—as he.

She may have been the smallest of the combined members of the Benedict, Jessop, and Kendall families, but by God, she was the mightiest.

Her name was Katherine Wesley Benedict, Josh's grandmother, and she was the undisputed head of the families.

"Just keep your shirts on, people. That especially applies to the ladies among us. This meeting isn't over until *I* say it's over."

His sister Susan was the first to recover. "Grandma Kate! You're back!"

Once that dam burst, everyone started calling out greetings and getting in line for hugs from the oldest and most loved—and, not coincidentally, the most feared—member of the Lusty Town Trust.

Josh joined that line, of course, because he loved his Grandma Kate almost more than he loved his own mother. Every time he put his arms around her, like now, he was mindful that she was getting older, and that her bones, if not her spirit, were becoming more delicate with each passing year.

"I'm so glad you're here," she told him as she patted his face.

He didn't hear that sentiment directed to any other member of the family. With his chest puffed out, he returned to his seat.

Grandma Kate received the last hug and then made her way to the head of the table, where Joshua's father, Caleb, held his chair for her.

Then Grandma Kate looked at Josh, and then Alex. "This is a very difficult time to be in the oil business, isn't it?"

Josh raised one eyebrow and looked over at his brother. They hadn't shared with anyone in the family the nasty letters they'd been getting in the last month. It simply defied comprehension how Grandma Kate could always know so much about what was going on in everyone's life. After all, there were so many of them!

"One company behaves irresponsibly, causing ecological devastation," the matriarch continued, "and we're all tarnished with that same brush."

"There's no question that share prices have dropped some," Uncle Carson, the former CEO of Benedict Oil and Minerals said. "But since share prices have dropped for every company, across-the-board, there doesn't seem to be much we can do about it."

Grandma Kate tilted her head to the side. "My immediate concern isn't share prices." She looked at Josh, and then again at Alex. "My immediate concern is demonstrating to the public at large that the Benedicts aren't like those other big, multinational conglomerates. Spoiling our environment is most definitely *not* the Benedict way. I want the world to know that, and the sooner, the better."

"Son, is something going on with the company that you'd like to share with the rest of us at this time?"

Josh resisted the urge to wince and close his eyes. His father Caleb was retired from the Texas Rangers, but being retired didn't mean a damn thing. The man was a cop down to the bone. He could put two and two together faster than even he himself could, and Josh had been a math scholar.

When denial is impossible, downplay. "There have been a few letters in recent weeks—you know how it is. Being a large company sometimes makes you a target. And when things go wrong, such as the recent disaster in the gulf, well, then, the target gets a bit bigger."

"Damn, boy. I swear you ought to run for political office," Uncle Carson said.

"Carson, watch your language," Grandma Kate said. "There are ladies present."

"Sorry, mother." Carson looked sorry, too.

"So, there've been threatening letters. I trust you've alerted Houston PD," Caleb said.

Alex sat forward. "No, sir. Josh and I felt that since the letters were more rants than actual threats, we'd just give it some time to blow over. We did, of course, give them over to our head of security. He also felt they weren't particularly immediate. One thing we can be pretty certain of is that at some point in the near future, some other company will earn the derision of the public. The blogospheres will explode, and our letter writer will have a new target."

"You hope," Jonathan, their other father, said.

"Yes, sir," Josh said. "We do hope."

"Waiting for something to not happen isn't the Benedict way, either," Grandma Kate said.

Since she was directing her steely gaze at him, Joshua swallowed and said the only thing a smart grandson could say. "No, ma'am, you're absolutely right. It's not. I apologize."

Grandma Kate considered him for a moment longer, then nodded.

"Since you brought it up, Mother, you must have something in mind to set this situation to rights." Jonathan said, and for a moment, Josh had a sense that his father had been reciting a line. He flicked a look at Alex, wondering if his sibling had the same sense. But Alex's gaze was on their grandmother.

"As it happens, I do." She took a moment to make eye contact with each member of the family—Benedicts, Jessops, and Kendalls—sitting around the table. This wasn't, by any means, the entire membership of the Lusty, Texas Town Trust. They'd become too numerous to sit down, all together, for the quarterly meetings. They all got together a couple of times a year, and needed the Lusty Community Center—a fairly new facility that could hold five hundred—for those events. No, these were the members elected by the Trust at large to serve as the oversight board. The term was for two years, and Josh and Alex were nearing the midway point of their first term.

"In order to show that Benedict Oil and Minerals, and by extension the Benedict, Kendall, and Jessop families, is proactive, I suggest we hire an environmental consultant. This consultant would report directly to this board, but would work closely with Josh and Alex. Every project, every site, every well, every mine, under the aegis of the family—past and present—will undergo a thorough environmental assessment. Where we are found lacking, ladies and gentlemen, we will remediate."

Uncle Carson, the one man Josh thought bold enough to protest both the intrusion and the expense of bringing in an outsider, sat back in his chair, puffed out a big breath, and said, "Mother, that's absolutely brilliant! We can get started right away, looking for the best candidate for the job."

Crap. The last thing that Josh wanted was someone sticking their nose in on every damn thing. Especially now, when he and Alex had initiated the Legacy Project.

"There's no need to do that," Grandma Kate said. "I've already located the best candidate for the job."

* * * *

Penelope Primrose blinked as she looked at the photograph on the museum wall and tried to quell the butterflies in her stomach. There was no reason whatsoever for her to feel nervous. Completely out of character for her, this sense of anxiety was as annoying as it was unexpected. *Best just pretend it doesn't even exist.*

So she refocused on the image before her, a historical photograph showing a group of people sitting together on blankets on a lawn. Unlike so many old portraits she'd seen of subjects looking stern and unyielding, everyone in this photograph was smiling. Reading the caption, she felt one eyebrow go up. Seated before the camera were Benedicts, Jessops, Kendalls, and two rather famous figures from the old West.

Not that she'd doubted her grandmother's best friend, no, not at all. It just seemed surreal to be here, in Lusty, Texas, a place that had captured her imagination since the first time she'd heard the stories of its founders so many years before.

Especially in recent years, Penelope had simply assumed the stories were a way that a very nice lady had tried to make her feel less afraid and alone when she'd come to live with her Grandmother Wright. Those tales Kate Benedict—who insisted on being called *Grandma Kate* instead of Mrs. Benedict—had told the ten-year-old, frightened child she'd been did help ease her sense of helplessness, and gave her something more, beyond herself, to think about. She'd imagined what it would have been like to have been sold into marriage by a greedy father and then have to travel across wild and untamed land. That had been a fate worse than her own lot. Oh, yes, the stories of the Benedict forebears and the founding of a town had not only comforted her loneliness, they'd fired her imagination, too.

How else to describe those wispy, sensuous dreams she'd had since she'd come of age? They had to have been the by-product of Grandma Kate's stories.

Until this moment, Penelope had never really believed those stories. Looking at the pictures of characters whose names she knew as well as her own, she could not deny the evidence before her. Every tale Grandma Kate had told her about Lusty, Texas, was true.

I should be feeling surrounded by the familiar.

Instead, she felt as if she stood on the precipice of something totally strange and unknown. Standing there, looking at a group photo that included the legendary Bat Masterson and Wyatt Earp, Penelope couldn't decide if this was a good kind of feeling or a bad one.

Piffle. It'll be the good kind, of course. She grinned. Her Grandmother Wright's favorite word edging into her thoughts helped to settle her. Piffle, indeed. This job was the break she'd been hoping for, the chance to earn a good salary doing the kind of work she'd trained long and hard for, the kind she'd spent so much time doing as a volunteer. Not only that, it was the change she needed, just when she needed it.

Penelope had studied environmental sciences, not just as a career choice, but as a passion. She had come to believe, with all her heart, that it was possible to marry economic and environmental goals. She'd never bought into the theory that all progress and business was bad for the environment, nor that all things good for the environment were bad for business. She did believe changes needed to be made. But for entrepreneurs who were concerned about the Earth, she knew there were moneymaking green technologies out there, waiting to be discovered, developed, or invested in.

The sound of steps approaching had her turning around. *My goodness, she looks like Sarah Benedict!* Of course, Penelope knew it couldn't be Sarah. In fact, now that her brain decided to join her, she had a suspicion she knew who the pretty young woman smiling at her was.

"Ms. Primrose? Hi, I'm Susan Benedict."

"Just Penelope, please. You look like your ancestor."

Susan's smile grew wider. "I know. I think it's kind of cool, myself. If you're ready, Grandmother asked that you join us, now."

"Certainly."

Penelope followed the young woman, not at all pleased that those butterflies that had mostly calmed had taken flight once more.

Susan Benedict waited beside the door and gestured her forward. Penelope inhaled deeply and entered the conference room.

Good heavens, there certainly were a lot of them! Penelope estimated that there had to be a good twenty people in the room, seated around the tables that had been set in a quadrangle. Her eyes fastened on the one person she knew and felt fairly comfortable with, Grandma Kate. She knew she was smiling because her face was beginning to feel stiff.

Since the two gentlemen on either side of Kate Benedict seemed to be regarding her with great attentiveness, she nodded to them. *Likely the oil executives.* In the few seconds that had lapsed since she'd entered the room, her mind chose the opportunity to ask a question she probably should have asked before now.

With all the rich details of the stories Grandma Kate had told her, why had she been so laconic about the family members in charge of Benedict Oil and Minerals?

"There you are, Penelope," Grandma Kate said. The elderly woman got up from her seat at the far end of the table and came toward her. "Thank you so much for waiting. Everyone, this is the environmental consultant you've all just voted to hire."

Grandma Kate reached her and put a comforting hand on her back. "Penelope, this motley crew is some of my family. I'm sure you'll meet them all and be thoroughly confused later, at dinner. But for now, I'd like to introduce you to the men you'll be working most closely with. Gentlemen?"

Chairs scraped the floor as two men, one sitting on each side of the room, stood.

"Penelope, this is Joshua and Alexander Benedict, two of my grandsons, and the current head honchos of Benedict Oil and Minerals."

Oh, dear. It wasn't the older men who had risen their feet, but two younger ones whose faces she hadn't seen when she entered as they'd been sitting, heads down, and writing. Her eyes fastened on two of the most handsome, well-built, yummy-looking men she had ever seen in her life. But that wasn't what had her heart pounding and those butterflies doing somersaults.

It was the sudden realization that there, standing before her, were the very images of the wispy, ethereal lovers who had haunted her dreams for the past six years.

Chapter 2

"Um...I wonder if you can tell us a little about yourself? That is, your past positions? I mean, of course, your experiences...as an environmental consultant?"

Penelope felt the heat of Joshua Benedict's gaze on her and wondered that she didn't melt into a puddle right then and there. Judging by his demeanor, and the way he'd just tripped over his words, he was as jolted by her as she had been by him and his brother. Never had she experienced such a reaction to the male of the species.

She knew there were a whole lot of people in the suddenly-too-small boardroom, but at the moment, the only ones she seemed to even register were those two honchos.

Don't stand there like a bleeding idiot. Answer the man.

How disconcerting to have her inner voice sound like the English waif she'd been as a child.

"Certainly. I graduated from Carnegie Mellon University, with an advanced degree in Civil Engineering and Environmental Sciences. I've spent the last two years working with the Kensington Foundation in Connecticut. It's a nonprofit foundation researching various green technologies and the interaction of those technologies with the natural habitats of the local flora and fauna. We were able to prove that a number of the new industries were able to coexist with these habitats without any negative side effects."

"So you're not interested in shutting down industries that have in the past proven detrimental to the environment?"

That question came from an older man sitting three seats down from Alex Benedict. He looked familiar to her, but several of these people did, since they were related to Kate. Then he smiled. "I'm sorry. I'm Carson Benedict."

One of Grandma Kate's sons. "No, sir. People need industry as much as they need a clean environment. I happen to believe there can be a marriage of the two principles. However, industry does have to be accountable, and do that which is right, not just that which is expedient. At the same time, I believe that environmental scientists must also be mindful of the needs of industry."

"People." Kate got to her feet and immediately commanded attention. Penelope resisted the urge to smile. The elderly woman was small, but by golly, one word from her and everyone looked at her, waiting.

When I grow up, I want to be just like her.

"I've got Penelope's full dossier that I will be happy to distribute to you. In addition, perhaps I should have mentioned that I've known her since she was ten, and that her grandmother was my good friend, Eloise Wright."

Penelope's throat tightened at the mention of her grandmother. That good woman who'd raised her had only been gone a few months. Looking at the faces around the table told her that was a fact with which they all seemed to be acquainted.

"Let's go have some dinner over at Kelsey's," Kate said. "I'm starving."

A man dressed in a khaki-brown uniform jumped to his feet. "F..phooey. I'd better let Kelsey know she's about to be inundated."

Grandma Kate laughed. "Relax, Matthew. I believe your mother has already notified your bride of the impending family invasion. And *now*, the meeting is over."

Kate was immediately swamped by her family, each one of them obviously glad to see her back home. Penelope sighed, grateful to no longer be the center of attention. One of the older men whom she'd originally pegged as an oil executive approached her.

"I'm Caleb, one of Kate's sons." He offered his hand. Penelope had heard of Caleb, of course, named for his great-grandfather.

She shook his hand. "I'm pleased to meet you. I've heard a great many tales from your family history."

Caleb smiled. "I suppose I should fess up and say I've heard about you, too. Mother always looked forward to visiting you and your grandmother. She took her passing hard. I'm sorry for your loss."

"Thank you. I feel very fortunate to have had my gram." Penelope swallowed the tears that still threatened from time to time.

"It's only a short walk to my daughter-in-law's restaurant," he said. "Why don't we head on over. Mother will be there, shortly."

Before she could answer, she felt a peculiar heat curl through her, touching off tiny embers that teased her female bits. She inhaled, and the scent of something very appetizing nearly made her mouth water.

In her peripheral vision, she saw that both Joshua and Alex had approached, and stood, one on either side, just behind her.

"That's a good idea, Dad," Joshua said.

Penelope turned so that she stood nearly beside the senior Benedict.

"Perhaps we'll have the opportunity to get to know each other as we walk," Alex said. "Since we're going to be working together."

Why did that sound like a threat? Penelope swallowed and decided to brazen it out. She stuck out her hand to Josh. "How do you do, Mr. Benedict?" She shook hands with the man, but was unable to hide her reaction to the zing she felt at his touch. "And you, Mr. Benedict?" The effect of Alex's hand in hers was no less potent, or disturbing, than his brother's had been.

"Don't be so formal. It's Josh and Alex," the latter said. "Since, as I said, we *are* going to be working so closely together, and all."

"Of course." For the first time, Penelope decided that brazening things out wasn't necessarily always the best policy. She could only hope that at the restaurant, she'd be able to keep her distance from these devastatingly arousing men.

* * * *

Alexander Benedict had never felt so off-kilter in his life.

He wanted to lay the blame for this feeling right at the dainty little feet of his Grandma Kate, but he wasn't even really certain that it was her fault.

A gentle, feminine laugh rippled across his skin, making his cock twitch and begin to harden. Beside him, his best friend and closest sibling, Joshua, sucked air in through his teeth and adjusted his position on the restaurant chair.

Alex didn't have to ask Josh if he'd just gotten a hard-on, too. He knew he had. There could be only one explanation why he and his sibling were both under this particular spell, reacting this way to a woman they'd met for the first time just a few hours before.

Penelope Primrose was a witch!

Though, with that deep black hair that almost sparkled blue in the lights and those violet, fathomless eyes, she could have played the role of a Greek goddess instead of a witch.

Aphrodite, naked, rising from the water, arms opening slowly in a lovers' welcome.

Whoa! Where the hell had that image come from? Alex dislodged the phantom of an old dream and focused his will on telling his cock the lady in question was definitely off-limits.

He watched her now, on the other side of *Lusty Appetites*, as she chatted with his sister-in-law Kelsey, the two of them behaving like old friends.

"Not hungry, son?" his father Jonathan asked.

Alex looked up at his dad, then down at his plate, still half full of Kelsey's delicious roast beef, fries, and gravy.

"Of course I am. I just didn't want to wolf down this great food and hurt Mother's feelings." Alex gave his fathers and his mother—

the three of whom sat across the table from him and Josh—a big smile.

His mother's response to that declaration was to raise one eyebrow, a look Alex knew well. Bernice Benedict was the queen of patented looks. That one small gesture said, *Who do you think you're trying to pull one over on?*, and was a look that she'd used on him many times in his life.

Then his mother shook her head. "I wonder which ancestor that smooth tongue and quick wit of yours comes from?"

"Darling, our son is one of a kind," his father, Caleb, said.

Alex could only grin back at his parents. He wasn't about to let a temporary aberration, and surely that's all this reaction he was having to Penelope Primrose could be, get in the way of his enjoying this unexpected family celebration. Good company, good food, and his Grandma Kate back in the bosom of their family, at least for the next few weeks, made for a very good evening, probably even better than the one he and Josh might have with luscious Lola. It was a comfort to think so, in any event.

Alex surveyed all the familiar people jammed into Kelsey's restaurant. It didn't take much to get the combined Benedict, Jessop, and Kendall families in the party mood, but nothing worked better than having their globe-trotting Grandma Kate back home.

The guest of honor was busy making the rounds, of course, moving from table to table, chatting, hugging, laughing. He didn't know where she got her energy. "Isn't she something?" He couldn't keep the admiration out of his voice.

"You'd never know she was ninety," his mother agreed. "I hope I'm half as active at her age."

Grandma Kate was clearly on a course that would bring her their way. She stopped at the table occupied by the rest of his siblings. He grinned when Colt and Ryder practically jumped to their feet. He guessed tales of his grandmother had preceded her, courtesy of his sister Susan, their future wife.

It was always such fun watching people and their first encounter with his grandmother. Anyone who thought to treat her like the proverbial "little old lady" was always in for a surprise.

Katherine Wesley Benedict was *nobody's* little old lady.

The door to *Lusty Appetites* opened, and Alex caught the flash of two uniforms, one a sheriff's brown and the other an Air Force captain's blue.

"My, my, I love a man—or two—in uniform!" Grandma Kate said.

Adam Kendall, Lusty's sheriff, and his brother Morgan both broke into wide grins.

"Kate!" Morgan made it over to her first. He scooped her up into his arms and spun her in a big circle. Alex winced, but his grandmother laughed like a young girl.

Morgan set her down and gave her a big, smacking kiss on the cheek. "It's about time my favorite girl came home to me."

"Oh, you. The two of you should be finding your own woman," she said, including Adam in that appraisal.

"Working on it," Adam said, just loud enough so that those close by could hear.

Alex grinned. That was the perfect answer to give Grandma Kate! Alex immediately adopted the stance as his own. As long as she had some indication that he was on the road to doing what she wanted him to do, she'd leave him be. She wouldn't even necessarily pester him for the details.

Alex turned to look at his brother.

"Adam's smart," Josh said quietly. "He headed her right off."

"I was just thinking that very thing myself. We'll keep that response on the ready for when she gets around to us."

Alex didn't think it would be a question of if, but when, she got around to them. Many of the nation's seniors adopted a cause in their December years. Grandma Kate's cause was marrying off as many of her grandchildren—both actual and associate—as possible, and as soon as possible.

"Morgan, come and sit down here. It's been so long since I've seen you." Grandma Kate grabbed the big man's hand and pulled him over to their table. Alex and Josh shifted to make room for them both.

"What have you been doing?" Grandma Kate lowered her voice to a loud whisper. "Or can you say?"

"Sorry, Kate. I really *can't* say." Morgan was a captain in the Air Force. Though he was a pilot, his current assignment was Special Tactics and Combat Control—or what was sometimes referred to as black ops. "But I've put in for a transfer to finish up this tour. I'll be doing something different soon. I'll be working on writing some training programs, which is really all I can say about that, too."

"Mom's glad because he'll be closer to home," Adam said. He came and stood just behind Grandma Kate's chair. "He'll be stationed at Goodfellow AFB over in San Angelo," Adam said.

Alex noticed that Adam stood so that he had his back to the wall and could see the entire restaurant. His own father did that sometimes. He guessed once a lawman, always a lawman. Though Alex couldn't understand why his cousin would need to feel so vigilant in his sister-in-law's restaurant in their own hometown. Alex's gaze strayed back to Penelope.

The woman moved with a fluid grace. He wondered how far down her back that gorgeous hair would fall if he snuck up to her and pulled the pins out. Would she taste sweet, like honey, or sharp and tangy, like his favorite hot salsa?

"Alexander."

Alex blinked. "Grandmother." He guessed his grandma had called his name a couple of times. He could feel his cheeks heating and wished for one moment the floor would open up and swallow him. *I wonder why, when we're embarrassed, we always wish for something that has never actually happened to anyone, and that, if it did happen, would likely hurt like hell?*

Alex blinked again and gave his grandmother his best smile.

"I'm going to rely on you and Joshua to give every bit of hospitality, assistance, and cooperation to Penelope that you can. Since the two of you *are* the honchos of our oil company, now, it's your duty to see to her. This project is very important to me."

Alex's radar quivered. He looked over at his brother. Josh returned his look, one eyebrow raised. That look told him he and his brother were on the same page.

Rather than wonder about it, he said, "Why is it so important to you, Grandma?"

"This last cruise I was just on, there was a young man on board who had a lot to say about big oil companies and what they've done to the planet. I wanted to boast about our ecological record, only I couldn't, not with any real authority. Made me feel uncomfortable. And it made me think that maybe we haven't been as good at global stewardship as we could have been. I do not like to feel uncomfortable, and I don't like to feel guilty." Then she lowered her gaze so that she looked at him over the top of her glasses. "And then there're those letters. They seem like threats to me, and no one threatens my grandchildren and gets away with it."

Of course, her answer made perfect sense. "Don't worry, Grandma. We'll both do everything we can to see that Penelope has everything she needs."

"Good. Susan and her men are heading out in a few minutes, on their way to pick up the boys' adopted father and bring him here. He's going to be staying with your folks. Did you know that your father Caleb knows Mike Murphy? Anyway, she offered Penelope her place for the night. The poor girl's been traveling since dawn. There's lots of room in that ranch house for the three of you. Tomorrow, y'all can head on out to Houston. You'll see she gets settled, both tonight and tomorrow?"

Alex looked at Josh. Neither one of them could deny their grandmother anything, even though, in this case, Alex wondered how he was going to possibly resist temptation. Spending the night in the same isolated ranch house as the beautiful Ms. Primrose? God help them all.

Since the lady in question had barely looked their way since they'd all come over to the restaurant, maybe it wouldn't be as difficult as he thought. Alex nodded. "Of course, Grandma. Josh and I will take very good care of Ms. Primrose."

* * * *

Penelope wasn't certain how it had happened, but after dinner, she found herself waving good-bye as Grandma Kate was driven off, while standing on the sidewalk as her luggage was being loaded into a Hummer.

A Hummer that belonged to Josh and Alex Benedict.

She'd done a pretty good job, she thought, avoiding the two devastatingly attractive men. When she shook hands with them after the meeting, felt her nipples peak and her slit leak, that had been her only option. Avoid them, avoid temptation.

Joshua and Alex Benedict are not *the men that have visited my dream-time sexual fantasies for the last six years.*

It didn't matter how many times Penelope played that mantra through her mind. Her body wasn't paying any attention to her. No, at this very moment, her hot little hormones were doing a happy dance up and down the outside of her pussy.

"It's not far to Susie's place," Alex said. "She's taken over and remodeled an old ranch house at the north end of the original Benedict tract."

Penelope had been scrambling for some way to get her mind off her arousal and could have wept with joy over this conversational offering.

"The original ranch that Sarah Benedict inherited from that blackguard, Tyrone Maddox?" she asked.

Alex's eyes widened, and Josh said, "You know about our family history?"

"Oh, yes. Your grandmother and mine were good friends for years, remember. After I went to live with my Grandma Wright, your Grandma Kate was a regular visitor. She told me such stories about your ancestors." Penelope was on a roll. When Josh went to get behind the wheel of the vehicle and Alex stood with the front passenger door open for her, she got into the truck, then slid over to the middle of the large seat. *Keep talking.* "What a pleasure it was for me today to tour your museum while I waited to be called into the meeting. I felt as if I knew every one of the people whose portraits I viewed."

"So you do know about our family and our town? Our…traditions?" Alex's breath fluttered her ear as he expanded on Josh's question. His words were spoken in a tone Penelope could only describe as sexy.

When had he moved so close to her? What in the name of all that was holy was she doing in the front seat of this truck, between these two extremely studly men, watching the lights of the town of Lusty fade away into the background?

She looked at Alex, then over at Josh. Both men were looking at her as if they hadn't eaten in a lifetime and she was a feast for their own personal consumption. The interior of the truck seemed to shrink, was suddenly impossibly small. Their masculine scent, raw and appetizing, went to her head faster than the most expensive champagne ever could.

Her pussy cheered, and her brain began to short-circuit. She blinked, tried to remember the question Alex had just asked her at the same time she realized Josh had put the turn signal on and was slowing the vehicle, then pulling over to the side of the road.

"Um…er…yes…Oh, God, what was the question?" Penelope wanted to cringe at the weak, whispery sound of her words.

"Perfect answer." Alex's words brushed her face seconds before his lips claimed hers.

Lusty and luscious, wet and wild, Alex's mouth covered hers. His flavor tantalized, hot and delicious. His tongue wooed hers, and then conquered it with motions at once seductive and dominating.

Alex raised his head, eased back, and Penelope had one moment to blink and another moment to recognize the sensation of another arm coming around her, a gentle hand turning her head.

Josh's kiss was every bit as destroying as Alex's had been, his flavor different yet just as potent. His tongue, bold and bodacious, penetrated her mouth again and again, and Penelope's mind came to life just long enough to make her think of what else might soon penetrate her wet and willing self, again and again.

She managed to break the kiss and throw herself against the seat back. Closing her eyes, she fought for breath. "This is a mistake," she said.

Both men inhaled then exhaled deeply.

"You're right. It is," Alex said.

It was?

"Absolutely a mistake," Josh said.

Well, hell.

"And it's a mistake that is about to not only be repeated but extrapolated upon as soon as we get to Susie's place." Alex's voice had dipped, deep and dark, and Penelope shivered.

The man had used the word "extrapolated." There was absolutely no doubt about one more thing, and she was honest enough to admit it, if only to herself.

Penelope was toast.

Chapter 3

Hurry, hurry, hurry!

Josh blinked, not knowing if he'd said the words aloud or not, and at that exact moment in time, he didn't even care. He'd stopped the Hummer as close to Susan's front door as he could manage. By the time he'd slammed the driver's door closed and rounded the hood, Alex had Penelope out of the truck, wrapped in his arms, and was kissing her.

As soon as Josh stepped close, his brother relinquished the woman to his arms. He set his mouth on her, famished for another taste, since the first had been so heady and intoxicating, his mind had almost convinced him he'd imagined it.

Not imagination. He drank from her, his tongue imitating another kind of drinking, and his cock stretched, hot and hard and ready to plunder.

"My suitcase," she said as he raised his mouth and passed her back to Alex.

"Don't need it." Alex's words tapered off against her mouth. They all took a couple of steps closer to the front door. Then Josh got his hands on her again.

Josh kissed her, his fingers moving to touch all of her at once, a single long caress from ass to breasts to pussy—*my God, the heat of her*—and then back to her ass to pull her close and rub her against his randy cock. He didn't stop to think about anything, not the speed with which this was happening, or the lack of planning, hell, the lack of everything. One millisecond of reason surfaced, shouted *condoms!*, then disappeared when Josh remembered whose house—whose *bed*—they were about to hit.

In his sister's house, there should not only be condoms in the bedside table, but likely all over the damn house. He gave Penelope back to Alex and turned to open the door.

"Clothes," Penelope said before Alex reclaimed her mouth.

Josh couldn't help himself. Once they were inside the house, he pressed his front against her back. She was still sucking face with Alex, so Josh ran his hand, his *shaking* hand, up and down her back.

"We'll get your bag inside in the morning, sweetheart. You won't need any more clothes until then," he said.

Penelope pulled her mouth away from Alex's, rubbed her cheek against the hand Josh had laid on her shoulder, and said, "This is crazy! Insane! What the hell are we *doing*?"

"We're feasting on you, Penelope, and very shortly we'll be fucking you. If you don't want this, say so now. Do we go upstairs and get naked? Yes or no?"

Two seconds felt like two hundred as Penelope blinked, owl-like, and looked from him to his brother.

"Yes." And then, "Yes, yes, yes. Oh, God, I'm *so* horny. I've never been so horny. You've cast a spell on me, the two of you. *Hurry*."

"Hang on, baby, we'll take care of you," Joshua said. He spun Penelope around and scooped her into his arms. The sound of his pounding heart competed with the sound of his and his brother's pounding footsteps as they ran up the stairs.

And then they were in the bedroom, the beautifully renovated master bedroom complete with a Benedict-sized bed and—please, God—a condom-bearing nightstand.

Joshua set Penelope down, then cradled her face in his hands. "You're so damn tasty. I can't seem to get enough of you. And you're not the only one who's horny. I just hope we can hold off long enough to pleasure you." He needed to sip her again. His mouth covered hers, his tongue voracious now, and as he pulled her into his arms, his hard cock nestled low on her belly. Her hips surged into his, telling him she burned as hotly as he did.

He felt Alex close, understood his brother was touching her, petting her, rubbing his own engorged cock against her hip. Never had the two of them been so instantly and completely captivated by a woman before, and never had it felt so *right*.

Joshua stepped back, handed Penelope over to Alex, and went in search of those condoms. He hit the jackpot in the first drawer he opened, spying the condoms and much, much more. *My God, everything we could ever ask for is in here.*

"Let me." Alex's voice drew his attention. "I've been fantasizing," his brother said as he reached up and began to draw the pins from Penelope's hair.

Miles of black, luminous locks tumbled free, cascading down to hang just at the middle of her sweet, sweet ass.

"Jesus." Alex's one word, reverent, as he gently combed his fingers through her hair, echoed Josh's sentiment, exactly.

"My God." Like a man mesmerized, Josh tossed the condoms onto the table and went to her.

He cupped her face, turned her to him, and kissed her again at the same time his brother started liberating her from her clothes.

Josh's hands shook anew as he helped undress her, as her body emerged, impossibly creamy flesh, soft and smooth and hot, drugging in its allure. Her breasts, full, pink-tipped, begged his hands to cup and caress them. Her waist dipped sensuously, womanly curves flaring to hips that would cradle him and a wonderfully bare pussy calling his name.

"Please." The anxiety in her plea damn near brought him to his knees.

This burning need, this spell, had not stricken them alone, had not only captured him and his brother. Theirs weren't the only trembles of need, or the only moans as hands explored naked, needy skin.

A man possessed, Joshua yanked off his clothes, discarded the coverings of society so he could press his flesh to hers, unsurprised to see his brother of the same mind.

They moved as one, and touched her, and kissed her, and brought her down to the bed.

* * * *

Oh, God.

Penelope had never hungered like this, never needed like this. It didn't make sense, it defied logic, when sense and logic had always been the cornerstones of her life from the time she turned ten.

Josh and Alex felt so hot, they seemed to burn, and she knew, she *knew,* somewhere down deep inside, that they burned this way only for her.

She kissed them, first one, then the other, mating her mouth to theirs, her lips sliding, sampling, tasting, *reveling* in the flavor and the arousal of lips on lips and tongues entwined.

Their hands began to learn her even as she set hers to explore their magnificent, flesh-covered muscles, the soft pelts of hair over pecs, then down, irresistibly down, to sweep over hard, vibrant, compelling cocks.

The heat of their bodies, as they sandwiched her between them, seeped into her, thawing parts of her she'd believed frozen forever. It was just sex, she knew it was just sex, and yet it felt like so much more. It felt like destiny.

"Please!" Was that her begging? She never begged. She exchanged. She indulged in tasteful, careful, civilized sex. Oh, God, there was nothing civilized about this at all!

"What are you doing to me?" Her mind's last attempt to bring reason to the situation fell victim to a breathless, feminine query.

"We're loving you, Penelope," Alex said. "We're just loving you."

She doubted he realized the word he'd used, and she was too far gone to think about it deeply. How could it be love when they'd only met? How could it be love when it felt so raw and untamed?

Joshua moved, reached out to the nightstand, then tossed something to his brother. "Which one of us do you want inside you first, baby?"

Lips and tongues, hands and bodies, kissed and licked, petted and pressed, and Penelope left reason behind as arousal soared and soared incredibly higher, turning greedy and needy and demanding.

"I don't care. I don't care. Just…oh, God, somebody fuck me!"

She sensed them moving, looking at each other, and the hesitation felt infinite as her body began to shake in desperation.

And then Joshua mounted her, his body pressing her into the mattress, his hands cupping her face, bringing her focus to him.

"Here, now. Take me. Take me, sweet baby." He laid his lips on hers at the same instant he thrust his cock all the way into her, balls deep.

Penelope wrapped herself around him and returned his thrusts, measure for measure, the stretching, the fullness, feeding her sudden frenzy, answering the call of a passion too rarely stirred.

She pulled her lips from his so she could kiss and lick his neck and whisper, "Good. It feels so good. More. Faster. Fuck me faster."

Then she took his mouth again, her tongue daring and bold as her hips continued to grind against his. Flames of passion exploded into a fiery conflagration as her orgasm erupted.

Fast and furious, the rapture flooded her, lifted her, and carried her away, far away from herself. Pure pleasure, bountiful bliss, the climax went on and on, a rich, full joy that slowly, oh so slowly, pooled into contentment.

So focused on her own sensations had she been, she'd barely noticed the man on her, in her, stiffening, shouting, and coming inside her.

As the stars behind her closed eyelids faded, tiny snippets returned, including the certain knowledge that he had indeed used a condom.

During the few times she'd had sex in the past, Penelope had always ensured there was a condom—she usually tucked one into her purse, just in case. Number one on her checklist of preparations, this time it had completely escaped her thoughts.

"I didn't hurt you?" Josh asked. He eased off of her and snuggled close on her right.

Penelope opened her eyes. He looked as wrecked as she felt. She'd never caused a man to look wrecked before. She'd believed she didn't have it in her. Apparently, she'd been wrong. Thank God. "No," she reached up and gently caressed his cheek, "you didn't hurt me."

Alex kissed her left shoulder, and she turned her head toward him. His mouth captured hers, his kiss sweet, wet and open, hot. He eased back and said, "You're incredibly gorgeous when you come."

Penelope felt flustered, which struck her as odd. *One would have thought if I was going to feel flustered, it should have been as they were waltzing me into the house to get laid.*

"Um…thank you. I think."

Alex's grin split wide open. "You're welcome." Then his expression turned lusty, and from just that one heated look, her arousal stirred anew.

She vaguely noticed that Josh slipped from the bed, but her focus stayed on Alex as he rose up, half over her, and began to work his own carnal magic on her body.

With a touch that felt infinitely gentle, he stroked her, neck to thigh, with long, lavish caresses. His attention seemed riveted to her as he petted and cupped. His gaze flicked up to hers. "I don't know what it is about you," he said quietly. "There's a part of me that feels as if I've known you forever. A part that feels as if I'm going to explode if I don't get inside you now."

He leaned over her and kissed her again, and this kiss tasted of that raw need. His tongue delved into her mouth again and again, hard and fast and deep. Penelope's passion grew. Her nipples hardened, and her slit leaked her juices so that she felt the dampness when her dew was brushed by the cooler air of the room.

The kiss tapered, and she said, "You taste different than Josh." She just said that and, for one instant, wondered if that had been some faux pas against ménage etiquette, but Alex just continued to touch her, arousing her slowly. His entire body seemed to be quivering slightly.

He said, "Good. That means you'll be able to tell us apart in the dark."

He swept his hand down, his fingers trailing a path of heat as he stroked her. At the top of her slit, he ran them back and forth over her clit, making that tiny bud quiver with excitement. She moaned. He smiled. Then he moved, fast as lightning, up and then down, and buried his face between her thighs and opened his mouth on her pussy.

"Oh, God!" Easygoing collapsed under his oral assault. Her passion poured out of her, this orgasm sudden, full, with no buildup, no warning, just wave after wave of ecstasy that made her cry out in delight.

Josh had come back to the bed, and he turned her face toward him and kissed her, as if he could drink her orgasm into himself. Then he eased back and Alex moved up her body and plunged his cock into her in one deep thrust.

"Oh, *yes*." She loved the sensation of being filled again, and the look on his face as he held himself still, eyes closed, told her he savored this first moment of joining. This was sexy and warmth combined. Why she would feel loved when they'd only met escaped her attempts at understanding.

Then he opened his eyes, and his deep-chocolate gaze locked with hers as he began to thrust in her, a slow, rocking rhythm that pushed her arousal higher and higher.

"Come with me, Penelope. Come again and fly with me." He leaned down and shared her flavor with her, kissing her with full openmouthed splendor. He scooped one arm under her and pressed her closer.

The taste of them, combined, created a savory essence rich and dark and somehow forbidden, yet oh, so compelling. She clamped on him, moved with him, and surrendered to the power of the pinnacle she shared with him as she came and came and came.

Chapter 4

Morning sun streamed across her face, and Penelope stirred, trying to escape the brightness that seemed to want to land right where her eyes were trying to sleep.

As she came to full wakefulness, she felt two solid walls of heat, front and back. Trapped on her side, images from the night before assailed her. Inhaling deeply, she took in the aroma of sex, and her hormones began to quiver.

Penelope's eyes fluttered opened, and she realized that somehow, during the night, she'd become the female filling for a man sandwich.

She'd never had enough practice at having a morning after to become good at the morning-after routine, but she thought this one might be slightly more awkward than most.

She'd just spent the night having rip-roaring, rocking sex with two of sweet Grandma Kate's favorite grandbabies, after having known said grandbabies less than a day!

"Good morning, Penelope." Sleep-husky and incredibly sexy, Josh's voice caressed her senses and her lips just before he leaned that little bit closer and kissed her.

Before she could fully respond to his greeting, she felt herself being eased onto her back, and Alex's "Good morning" reverberated against her mouth with his kiss.

He eased back and stroked his thumb over her bottom lip. "If you want to grab a shower, we'll have your suitcase up here for you before you're out," he said. "Bathroom's across the hall."

"We'll have breakfast ready, too," Josh said. "So when you're ready, just come on downstairs."

"Oh, um…" She really never got the chance to say anything because first Josh and then Alex kissed her again. This time their tongues reminded her of all the wonderful things they could do to her. These kisses, long, hot, and arousing, nearly had her grabbing the nearest man and pulling him onto her wet and willing naked body.

Before she could do something she'd likely regret, the men practically leapt from the bed. She had one moment to admire their beautiful naked asses and luscious, engorged cocks, which were standing at more than half-mast.

"We'd both like nothing better than to pick up where we left off, as you can see," Josh said.

"But we need to talk, sweetheart. So we'll see you downstairs," Alex said.

And then they scooped up their boxers and trousers and *left*.

Penelope had lifted her head and chest from the bed, wanting to spend every second possible ogling their sexy male selves, wanting very much to pick up where they'd left off the night before, wanting to put off *thinking* for as long as humanly possible.

She plopped herself back down flat on the bed and sighed. *Well, hell.* She guessed if she was going to have to eat and think and talk, she'd best take a nice, hot, bracing shower, first.

Mere minutes later, Penelope sighed in bliss. She opted instead for a bath and sank into the deep tub of hot, fragrant water. She'd almost given in to the hedonistic urge to indulge herself in the spa this fabulous bathroom held, but had changed her mind at the last moment and chosen this claw-foot tub instead.

This is just as good as the spa would have been. At least she told herself it was, especially for soaking away the tenderness she felt between her thighs and in her hips from the unaccustomed sexual activity. She did have a lot to think about, and not really a lot of time to do so. Fortunately, her ability to sort and select, to ponder, weigh, and consider—in short, her ability to utilize reason and logic—had returned with the morning sun.

What she needed to do, and needed to do immediately, was to decide how she wanted this episode of uncharacteristic libidinous excess to turn out. Did she want to simply write it off as one of those once-in-a-lifetime experiences that she would then tuck into a memory box? Or did she want more of the same?

Just thinking about more of the same had her juices flowing, her heart pounding, and her nipples standing at attention. "You be quiet, you randy hormones. You had your say last night. This morning, it's the brain's turn." She said that aloud but quietly, and trusted in the integrity of the closed door—crap, which she'd forgotten to close! *Well, I'm not going to get out and close it now. What would be the point?*

Penelope sighed again and lay back against the cool, white porcelain. When she examined all the facts and data, she realized she could potentially have a serious problem.

So she soaked, and she relaxed, and let her gifted, organizational-loving brain work on the matter.

The scent of coffee and bacon drifted up the stairs. Her tummy rumbled, so she told her brain to make it snappy.

* * * *

Joshua looked up as his brother came back down the stairs. "I don't hear the shower running," he said.

"She's having a bath." Alex said the words softly.

"Oh, God, the hot tub? *Fuck*, envisioning Penelope in the hot tub is not doing my cock any favors, brother."

"What you mean is, it's doing your cock lots of favors, but this morning your brain has something to say about that fact."

Josh laughed. "Yeah, that's what I mean all right." He turned the bacon in the frying pan, then added a half dozen sausages into it. "Never in my wildest dreams did I ever imagine a night like last night could happen to us."

"How could you have? How many women have we met, the two of us? I mean, Legacy Project aside. Just in the day-to-day scheme of things, ever since we figured out what those blessed little foil packages were for. How many, do you think? Fifty? Sixty?"

"Hey, we're not man-sluts," Josh protested.

"No, I didn't ask how many we've had sex with, just how many we've *met*."

"Just met? Hell, more than a hundred up to the end of university. Has to be more like a few hundred, and yeah, I get your point. Going off like that, hot and horny, on first meet—in short, zooming from zero to Mach 2 in seconds flat, yeah, that's one hell of an aberration, there."

"Probably a one in a kajillion chance, hormonally speaking, that such a thing would ever happen to us," Alex said.

"Yeah." Josh exhaled heavily. The sound of movement upstairs alerted him that pretty Penelope was out of her bath and getting dressed. Blotting the water from that incredible body of hers with one of his sister's big, fluffy towels…Josh shook his head and pulled his attention back to the conversation at hand.

"We have to handle this very carefully," Alex said. "I don't suppose you have any kind of prepared-ahead-of-time mental checklist for this sort of a situation?"

"Bro, I try to foresee most possibilities, but, hey, one in a kajillion? Not even *I* am that good."

The sound of a light step on the stairs shut Josh's mouth and turned his gaze back to the stove.

He took the bacon out, turned the sausages, then added the scrambled egg mixture to a second skillet.

"Good morning, gentlemen. Breakfast smells delicious," Penelope said.

Josh looked over his shoulder, gave the woman a smile. "Good morning. Have a seat. It's nearly ready." So far, so good. That greeting could have been between two people who'd parted at the top of the stairs the night before, not two who'd been all over each other, and more than once. A vision flashed, his hot, hard cock sliding so sexily into her wet, waiting cunt.

Focus, Josh, focus.

"I hope you like your eggs scrambled," Alex said. He saw Penelope seated at the table and then poured her a cup of coffee. "Because that's the only way Josh cooks them. Ever."

"Oh?" She looked at Josh, one eyebrow raised.

He turned his attention back to the stove to stir said eggs. "I read a report last year that said one in every seven hundred eggs is infected with the bacterium *Salmonella enteritidis.*"

"Rather long odds, if you ask me, but I suppose caution is reasonable," Penelope said.

"Not just reasonable, but mathematically sound," Josh said.

When she continued to smile at him, he took it as encouragement. "I like eggs and would, in any given week, likely eat as many as eight of them. Over the course of a year, that's four hundred and sixteen eggs. In a decade…well, you can see, odds of escaping unscathed are *not* in my favor. Hence, all the eggs I eat are thoroughly cooked."

"Well, lucky for me, then, that I do like scrambled eggs. I especially like scrambled eggs if the cook sprinkles cheese on them." She sounded hopeful.

"I have some grated cheddar right here. We, um, didn't know if you liked hot salsa with your eggs or not, so I haven't added any."

"I've never tried it. Perhaps I will, now that I'm in Texas."

"Grandma Kate said you're originally from England, but that you've been living in upstate New York since you were a kid," Alex said. "I guess too many years here made you lose your accent, huh?"

Penelope laughed. Josh noted that sound had nearly the same effect on him this morning as it had the night before, sort of like a soft silk scarf being brushed over his naked flesh kind of effect.

"Actually," she said, "I have learned to smooth it out, so to speak, and pardon the pun. However, if I set my mind to it—or when I'm extremely angry—then you'd think by the sounds of me I'd just jumped off the boat."

Amazing. Over the course of that one sentence, she'd let her voice change, just a subtle shift, and there was the most adorable English accent. Was it called a brogue? Josh made a note to look it up, later.

The food was ready, so Josh served it up onto a platter and brought it to the table. Alex added a pile of toast to the offerings, and both men sat, with Penelope between them.

"Good heavens, that is a lot of food," Penelope said. "I usually only have some fruit and yogurt each morning."

"Yogurt. That's the not-quite-cheese product with live bacterium swimming about in it?" Josh couldn't suppress his shudder. He'd been going to try the stuff once, until he heard about the "live cultures" in it.

Penelope laughed. "It is. And it's quite good, and good for you, too."

"I'll take your word for it," he said.

For the next few minutes, everyone focused on putting food on their plates and then in their mouths.

"Listen, Penelope. About last night." Josh winced, because those words weren't quite what he meant to say, and worse, they sounded like the beginning of a brush-off.

"Oh, oh. Is this the morning-after brush-off?" she asked.

"No! No," Alex replied. Josh ducked in response to the scathing look his brother sent him. "No, it's just…well, what happened last night…we've never done that before, and we didn't want you to think that we're a couple of…of man-sluts."

"Come now, gentlemen." Penelope frowned. "Or rather, don't come. Not right now, at any rate, breakfast table and food and all."

Josh and Alex both burst out laughing. Penelope simply smiled at them and waited for them to quiet down.

"What I mean to say is," she continued, "you were both entirely too good at giving me pleasure last night to have been virgins."

"*Virgins?* Hell, no, we weren't virgins!" Josh shook his head. "What *we* meant to say was that we don't usually have sex with a woman we've just met. And honestly, we *never* have sex with women who work for us."

"I don't actually work for you," she said. "I work for your family. I report to the Town Trust, in general," she paused and gave them a brilliant smile, "and Grandma Kate, in particular."

"Yeah, that's the other thing," Alex said softly. "We promised Grandma Kate we'd take good care of you."

Penelope picked up her coffee cup—to drink, or to hide the fact that she looked like she wanted to laugh at them? Josh couldn't say, but he did have his suspicions. He guessed he couldn't blame her. He and his brother weren't quite handling the situation in their most urbane, effective, or business-executive manner.

"If you like, I can write a testimonial to her on your behalf, with regard to how very well you *did* take care of me last night," she said. She gave Alex a sweet smile, and then she gave one to Josh.

Josh thought he could likely do anything in the world if, at the end of the day, he had one of her smiles as a reward.

"Let me put your minds at ease. I don't think you're man-sluts. I was a full participant in the fun and games last night. Something like that has never happened to me, either. Perhaps it was the full moon, or maybe an errant spell from a practicing witch in the vicinity. But no harm, no foul. As for our working together, that shouldn't be a problem. I'm very good at compartmentalization, and since you're both, as Grandma Kate calls you, the honchos of a major American corporation, I'm certain you are, too."

Man, she used the word "compartmentalization." Josh could have sworn his heart gave an extra little thump. He mentally shook his head and gave his butt a metaphorical kick.

"So…we're good, then?" Josh asked.

"I'd say you're very good. Excellent, even. And we're all on the same page, too," she said.

He laughed, and met his brother's gaze, but couldn't deny the funny little something running around in his head, giving sharp jabs to his conscience.

After a fumbling start, they'd ended up, conversationally, exactly where they needed to be. In just a couple hours, they'd be back in Houston, back at work, and back working to refine the Legacy Project. Now they could go ahead with those plans, as well as see to it that Penelope Primrose got settled in and set up.

Last night had been rapturous, exciting, and the best sex of their lives, but it was in the past.

"Great," Josh said.

And he spent the rest of his breakfast time trying to figure out why what should have felt great, didn't.

Chapter 5

Penelope tried not to gawk as Josh and Alex drove through the complex that was Benedict Towers in downtown Houston. When she'd been working to put herself through school, she'd worked on the hotel staff of the Carstairs Manhattan, one of the finest five-star hotels in the world. So she had seen opulence up close and personal before.

She just never thought to experience that lifestyle for herself.

Good God, when Grandma Kate said the family would set me up in an apartment, I had no idea it would be someplace like this.

Penelope never thought of her grandmother's best friend as being wealthy because Grandma Kate had always been just Grandma Kate. The woman had never put on airs, had always been what her own grandmother called "just plain folk."

Josh stopped his Hummer at the front door, and a doorman hurried forward to greet them.

"Good morning, Mr. Benedict."

"Hey, Carl, how's it going?" Josh asked.

"Just great, sir. Would you like me to park it for you?"

"Just in the short-term area, please. Carl, this is Ms. Primrose."

Carl turned his smile toward her. He tipped his hat and even offered her a slight bow. "Welcome to Benedict Towers, Ms. Primrose. We've been expecting you. Your car has arrived. When you want it, just call down and let us know, and we'll have it ready for you."

"Thank you, Carl." Car? Grandma Kate never said anything about a car. Her shock must have shown, because Josh sent her a big grin.

"You'd become poor very quickly taking taxis in this town. Houston is the fourth largest city in the nation, and covers approximately six hundred and sixty square miles," he said. "It was a simple enough matter to have one of the company vehicles available for your use while you're with us. Um…" He stopped and looked at her, his expression slightly sheepish. She thought he was about to apologize for running off at the mouth like a member of the Visitors and Conventions Bureau. Instead, he said, "You do have a driver's license, don't you?"

"Yes, I do. You'll want to take a photocopy of it for insurance purposes." Penelope very nearly reached into her handbag for the document right then and there.

"Stella, our admin, will see to that," Alex said. "Later today or tomorrow—whenever you come in to the office."

He walked around to the back and pulled her two suitcases out of the back. "Shall we?"

"After you," Penelope said.

The lobby of the building appeared as lushly furnished as she'd imagined such a place would be. Marble floors, rich leather furniture, and what appeared to be a front desk made of polished mahogany spoke of quiet elegance.

Rather than walking straight to the elevator, the brothers Benedict led her to the desk. There, a young woman dressed in a business suit, complete with red tie, greeted the men with a big smile.

"Good morning, sirs."

"Daphne." Alex smiled at her. "This is Ms. Primrose. Penelope, Daphne is a member of the concierge staff. If there's anything you need, she, or whomever is on duty here, can help you."

Concierge staff? It was on the tip of her tongue to ask if this was an apartment building or a hotel. The young woman's greeting robbed her of speech.

"Welcome, Ms. Primrose. Penthouse Three is ready for you. We have, of course, stocked it with some basic groceries and toiletries.

Here's the key, which is also the key for the elevator. If I can be of any assistance, simply dial eight on your phone."

"Thank you, Daphne." Penelope hoped she appeared gracious and not goggle-eyed.

She followed her suitcases, which just happened to be attached to Alex Benedict, to a bank of two elevators that was to the right of the concierge desk.

"A penthouse," she repeated, simply because she wasn't sure if she'd heard correctly.

"Penthouse Three. There are three in this, the north tower, and three in the other—the south tower."

"Surely you can't expect me to stay in a penthouse for the entire term of my contract?" My God, the cost of that was going to be astronomical.

"Two years *is* a long time to be stuck in an apartment," Josh agreed. "Just let us know when you get tired of it, and we'll move you to one of the condos."

"No, I meant I researched the cost of living in Houston before I arrived. I'd budgeted for a small, bachelorette apartment out in one of the suburbs."

"You're not paying for this, of course. Grandma Kate insisted that you stay here as her guest," Alex said.

"There's not a member of the Benedict, Kendall, or Jessop clan that can say no to Grandma Kate," Alex said.

I'm Alice, and I've fallen down the rabbit hole.

Josh showed her how to use the key for the elevator—she'd have figured it out because each keyhole was numbered. The doors opened, and they stepped in. In a shorter time than Penelope could imagine, they were on the penthouse floor.

"We're in Penthouse One, right across the hall, and various members of the family often occupy Penthouse Two," Alex said. "That's the one down there." He pointed to the left.

Josh handed her the key. Penelope inhaled deeply and then opened the door.

"Oh, good God. It's…it's beautiful." Drawn to the big windows, she moved into the living room, complete with plush carpeting in a soft gray, walls of eggshell, and furniture in stark white, with decorative pillows in teal and chartreuse. The view of the city stretched to the horizon. Penelope thought it would look magnificent at night.

Tongue-tied in the face of such luxury, she followed behind the men as they toured what would be her home for the next while, at least. The kitchen sparkled with stainless steel appliances and granite countertops.

And then they showed her the master bedroom.

"Do you think you'll be comfortable here?"

Alex had come up behind her while she stood and stared at the enormous bed. It had to be at least as large as the one they'd frolicked in last night at Susan's ranch house.

He set her suitcases down and then put his hands on her shoulders. Was that him shaking, or her?

"I…I…" Penelope's brain seemed unable to send a coherent sentence to her mouth.

"Maybe we should test out the bed, just to be certain it's to your liking." Josh came up to stand close beside her.

The heat from their bodies enveloped her. Their masculine scent, some mysterious fragrance she couldn't identify but loved, shot straight to her hormones.

Oh, this is so not a good idea. If she had any hope of keeping her heart safe from these two gorgeous men, she needed to pull back, and pull back *now*.

Alex's hands squeezed her shoulders then gently turned her around. Josh moved so that he stood nearly behind her, on her right. Their closeness set her blood to humming with sweet arousal, a drug she'd so rarely tasted in her life, its presence now simply enthralled her. Her mind scrambled for the words that would stop her from giving in. And then her body cried out, "But why?"

"Say yes, Penelope." Alex's head lowered, came closer. "We both need you. Say yes." The last two words bathed her lips with moist heat.

"Yes."

Alex's mouth covered hers, the touch of his lips gentle, wooing. His tongue caressed her bottom lip, and she opened to him, opened herself to whatever he wanted, whatever he needed.

His arms enveloped her, and she felt the ridge of his cock press against her. Deep inside her, her libido began to celebrate.

"Why do you both affect me this way?" She turned her head when Alex eased back so that her lips could mate with Josh's. His kiss, just as sweet, added to her growing passion. These two men fed her a sweet nectar that her body now, after just one night, craved.

"Chemistry. Pheromones," Josh whispered. "Mathematically, it's a one in a kajillion kind of reaction."

"Oh. Of course it is." Penelope closed her eyes and surrendered to the heat and the hunger pouring into her.

She turned her lips back to Alex, put her arms around his neck, and plundered. He tasted so good to her, all she wanted was more. Desire became a honeyed thickness that filled her veins and flooded her heart. Her pussy became unbelievably wet with her juices.

His arms around her held her close, and his hand began an up and down massage of her back and ass that weakened her defenses.

When Josh eased her out of Alex's arms, she turned to him eagerly, her mouth avid to taste and her tongue to dance with his. His hands explored her. His fingers sparked tiny fires where they touched, so that Penelope yearned for more.

She stepped back, just slightly. Her clothing had to go. It had become an intolerable barrier between her and what she craved more than her next breath.

The men must have felt the same way because they began to toss their own coverings aside, and they were a lot faster at it than she was.

"I need to take your hair down," Alex whispered. He stepped forward, and his body, hot, naked and so very near, nearly made her forget what she was doing.

His hands made quick work of pulling the clip and pins away. He simply dropped them on the floor then combed his fingers through her hair. "You are so gorgeous."

"I'm not." She stepped forward, unable to resist the lure of his strong neck and chest, her mouth suddenly watering for a taste of his magnificent male flesh.

"I'm the one doing the looking," Alex said. Then he lifted her face and kissed her, a deep, carnal kiss that made her clench her inner muscles in an attempt to keep her juices from escaping her.

"Let's finish getting you naked," Josh said.

His hand spread heat and lust as he stripped her bra and panties away. And then he pressed his back to her, rubbed his cock against her ass.

"We need to know what you like, baby," he said softly. "We want to make you feel good."

"Mm, anything. Everything. If you make me feel any better, I'm not sure I'll survive."

Josh's chuckle was low and rich and tickled her clit. "Trust me, sweetheart. This will never hurt you. *We* will never hurt you."

"I know." She could put what she really knew of these men in a thimble with room to spare, but she did know that.

Last night, they danced her to the bed in a ballet both graceful and sensuous. This morning, with daylight streaming through the bedroom window, she led the way to the enormous mattress with deliberate intent.

Just before Josh would have pressed her down onto the bed, she switched them so that his knees hit the edge of the thing first. The instant he sat, she lowered herself to her knees and took his cock into her mouth.

His surprised utterance ended on a groan, and he sucked in air and grabbed her head with both hands. Something in that action, the hint of domination, sent a zing of a thrill shivering through her. She moved her head on him, tasting him with her tongue as she ran it up and down his shaft, sucking gently. She kept her motions smooth, slow, and felt rewarded when he groaned and began to thrust his cock into her mouth. Alex stood close, and then closer, apparently absorbed in watching her suck his brother's cock.

She tasted his juices and knew he was close to the edge. Feeling brave and brazen, she slowly lifted her mouth from him, then turned and fisted Alex's stiff penis. "I don't want you to feel left out," she said, and then closed her lips around him.

His cock tasted just as good, if different, from Josh's. His moan of pleasure filled her with joy just as the flavor of him filled her with a hunger for more.

Each of them had a hand on her head. Those hands trembled slightly. She felt powerful as a woman and liked that feeling, a lot. She'd always believed herself ineffectual as a lover, and yet these virile men shook from her touch, from her mouth.

"Penelope, yes." Alex shivered, and bent over her just slightly as his hips rocked.

"Drink him, sweetheart," Josh whispered. "Take what he gives you."

Oh, yes, she wanted to taste him, she wanted to taste them both in this way. She brought her left hand up to gently cup Alex's sack. Up and down, in and out, she aroused him, and herself. Gently, then stronger, she sucked on him, caressed his balls, begging him to give her his hot, pungent gift.

"Oh, Lordy." Alex clutched her hair as the first stream of his release shot out of him. She received his seed, wrapping both arms around his ass as her mouth sucked it down, pulse after pulse of essence that tasted hot and salty and made her arousal soar.

He jerked and shivered with the force of his orgasm. *I did that for him.* That knowledge thrilled her, pleasured her in a way that was more than sexual, that warmed a special part of her woman's soul.

His cock softened, but not completely. He eased himself from her clasp and reached for her.

"Thank you." He kissed her, and the salute felt almost reverent.

"You're welcome." She nuzzled his neck even as Josh ran his hand from her hair, down her back, to her ass.

"My turn for exotic flavors," he said. When he turned her, she faced him. She opened her mouth for his kiss and ran her hands over his shoulders, down his arms. His flesh felt hot. When she fisted his cock, she found it hot and hard, the tiny eye atop it already oozing liquid.

Josh eased her hand away from him and pressed her body close. It felt so good to rub her breasts against the soft, light pelt covering his chest.

Alex stroked her back, and when he and his brother urged her onto the bed, she went. Alex stretched out on her left and gathered her hands in his and drew her arms above her head. His other hand he stroked over her breasts, tweaking her nipples, making her burn. Josh spread her legs and knelt between them.

"You're so beautiful. So lusty and generous. I need to taste you, too," he said.

Penelope watched as he lay down, as he cupped her ass and began to lick and kiss her inner thighs, gentle, teasing movements that made her shiver, made her wetter and hotter.

"Smells good." He whispered those words so close to her slit. She heard him inhale deeply, and she shivered, arousal sizzling along her nerve endings as she felt herself begin to climb.

Then he licked her, one long, broad stroke from her anus to her clit. Penelope gasped because that touch against her rosette shot an entirely different kind of heat through her.

"Mm, that's very promising," Josh said.

Then he closed his mouth over her cunt, his lips swirling on her, his tongue stroking inside her. Over and over and faster and faster, he licked, kissed, sucked, edging her arousal higher and higher. She felt him touch her with his fingers, and then he pushed them into her and found her G-spot. The combination of his mouth and fingers hurled her into the fire.

When he sucked her clit into his mouth, her climax overtook her, and she cried out as bliss rained over and in her, as her orgasm filled her up and emptied her out until she thought she'd melt right into the bed.

Chapter 6

Had there ever been a more beautiful day?

Alex whistled as he strode from his parking space in the underground parking lot to the elevator. He had a hell of a lot of work ahead of him, since he and Josh had ended up spending the rest of the afternoon and evening yesterday with pretty Penelope, rather than attending to business.

He supposed he might be in for a bit of tongue-lashing from Stella, their admin. *I wonder if that's really why Josh is coming in later.*

But no, Josh was taking a breakfast meeting with Andrea Martin, a member of the Chamber of Commerce and number two on the Legacy Project list. The meeting had been set up a few days before, and by the time Josh remembered about it, it had been too late to cancel.

Alex reviewed what he knew of Ms. Martin as he rode the elevator up to the top floor of the Benedict Oil and Minerals Headquarters.

The lady had graduated top of her class from Texas State University with a degree in Advertising and Mass Communication. She worked for a private ad firm in Dallas before relocating to Houston last year to take the position with the Chamber of Commerce. Her IQ was reportedly just shy of genius.

She liked camping and fishing, horseback riding and archery. In addition, she was an avid reader, and her motto, which she'd posted on her Every Face social networking page, was "Never stop learning, never stop growing."

She had most—but not all—of the qualities he and Josh had listed as desirable for the successful candidate for the Legacy Project.

In short, Ms. Andrea Martin would make them a good wife.

With the last of their siblings having become engaged just a month before, Alex and Josh had decided the time had come for them to get serious about finding a wife and domestic bliss for themselves. So they'd done what they did best—sat down and brainstormed the problem, with a view to finding a logical, practical solution.

The result was the Legacy Project, their pet name for the list they'd made of the candidates for the position of Mrs. Benedict.

So far they'd conducted a preliminary interview with just one candidate, luscious Lola Dell, a CPA with a high IQ and an unbelievable G-cup bra size. Alex had interviewed her at a breakfast meeting last week, and they'd made plans to have dinner with her the night before last.

He'd had to cancel that, of course, in light of his Grandma Kate's arrival home. *Maybe I should have sent flowers.* Alex shook his head. There'd be time to discuss strategy later, when Josh returned from his breakfast with Ms. Martin, and they discussed the next step.

The doors to the elevator opened to the executive floor. Five offices branched off from this central reception area like spokes of a wheel. One of the offices was in fact a conference room, which made attending meetings more efficient than if he and Josh had to go to separate floors, or, heaven forbid, across town. Only two of the remaining four offices were occupied full-time at the moment. The other two stood available to whichever family member—be they Benedict, Kendall, or Jessop—had need of them.

Alex smiled, for sitting at the enormous reception area, in true control of the Benedict empire, sat fifty-seven-year-old Stella Wyse, administrative assistant extraordinaire.

"Well it's about time one of you showed up," Stella said by way of greeting.

"Sorry, Stella. We had dinner the night before last with the entire family. Grandma Kate's back!"

"Yes, I know, Kate and I had lunch yesterday."

"Oh. Well, good. And I'm afraid Josh and I took more time than we'd planned on helping our new environmental consultant get situated—you know, new apartment, new car. I guess Grandma told you about hiring her."

Stella peered over her glasses at him in a way that reminded him of his grandmother. "Since I was the one to arrange for said apartment and car, yes, she did indeed tell me. Ms. Primrose, by the way, being the one new to town, car, and apartment, had *no* difficulty arriving by eight a.m. sharp. As per your grandmother's instructions, I've settled her in the blue office."

The blue office was one of the two spare executive offices on this floor. "Penelope's in?" He and Josh had both assured her, as they'd left her dozing in her bed that morning just shy of five, that they certainly didn't expect her to come in to work today.

"She is. And your father has commandeered the gray office, and has called a meeting of your security personnel, some department heads, and you and Josh for ten."

"My father's here?"

"He is, and asked to be notified, in his words, 'When my sons get around to showing up for work.'"

Alex flashed a grin. That quote told him which father had arrived, though of course he should have foreseen that he would.

He and Josh had deliberately not told any of the family about those letters they'd received so as to keep Caleb Benedict, Texas Ranger, retired, at home.

His fathers both needed a hobby, but of the two, Alex thought that Caleb needed it more.

"I'll go see Dad now."

"A wise decision. By the way, Kate thought that Ms. Primrose could use an admin of her own, since she is, in fact, a one-woman department."

"Good idea," Alex said. "If you could advise Human Resources, please…"

"Already done," Stella said. "She'll begin interviewing candidates in about a half hour."

"Wow. That's…great."

Stella smiled at him. "No need to waste time, is there?"

Since Stella had only repeated one of his grandmother's favorite sayings, Alex could only agree—despite the fact that something about the way she'd said that bothered him.

Stella's words also reminded him of the real reason why Josh was as yet absent. He hoped his brother's extended breakfast was a good sign.

"No," he said aloud, "there's no need to waste time." And with that, he directed his footsteps toward the office that held his father.

* * * *

Penelope knew as soon as the young man shook her hand that she'd found her administrative assistant. His name was Andrew Wildes, and since he'd been the first one mentioned as a candidate for the position by Mrs. Wyse—Stella—she gave a mental salute to the older woman's intuitive insight.

They clicked right from the first moment. Andrew had come to Texas two years before and had been raised in Albany, New York—only about fifty miles away from where she'd lived with her Grandma Wright.

As Penelope set out to get to know Andrew, she thought that, likely, Mrs. Wyse knew this company and the staff better, she'd wager, than those two hot honchos she'd spent the night with. Again.

I have got to get those two studs out of my thoughts, at least during working hours.

She hadn't lied when she'd told Josh and Alex, yesterday at breakfast, that she had no trouble compartmentalizing her life. She wished now she'd thought to tack on the word "usually" to that statement. She hated it when circumstance made a liar out of her.

Penelope brought her attention back to the young man who sat across from her at the round meeting table in a corner of her office.

Her office. Penelope certainly liked the sound of that, something she never would have guessed about herself.

"I see that you've spent some time in the public affairs-communications department here, as well as in accounting," she said. "Can you tell me what attracted you to such dissimilar jobs?"

"Actually, Ms. Primr—Penelope," he blushed, she guessed, because he'd forgotten her request that he call her by her first name, "there are similarities in the two disciplines. You need to be able to work in a methodical fashion, and with attention to detail, in both. Sometimes you need to think outside of the box, too, although not quite so much in accounting as in public affairs."

"If you've a good eye for detail, then I do believe you're my man."

"That's great. Brian—he's head of P.A. and communications—said that if you chose me I was to begin right away, as Mrs. Benedict has let it be known the work you're going to be doing is important to her. So, where do we start?"

Penelope blinked. It would seem that Grandma Kate had been busy since she'd been back. Funny, but when she'd offered Penelope the position, she hadn't indicated that she thought it would be such a big deal.

Probably didn't want to make me feel under pressure.

Penelope had already determined to do the very best job she could. Now she was doubly determined. "What I would like for you to assemble, please, is a list of every site, past and present, that has been developed by the company. My understanding is that the Benedicts tend not to sell land once the element in question has been extracted. So we're looking at a fairly extensive list, I would imagine."

To his credit, Andrew began to make notes as soon as she'd begun to speak.

"How far back do we go? Do we key our list after any specific legislation was passed?"

"No. We're doing this in-house, at the direction of the Benedict, Kendall, and Jessop families. My instructions were to leave no stone unturned, so we go back to the very beginning."

"The beginning?"

Penelope smiled. She thought that her personal knowledge of the family was going to come in especially handy now. "That's right. We begin with all the land that Sarah Carmichael Benedict inherited from Tyrone Maddox, and the very first oil well drilled by the Benedicts near the end of the eighteen-hundreds."

Andrew's eyes widened. "That is going to be a lot of properties, and a lot of different venues," he said.

"Yes, I know. So I guess we'd better get started." She looked at her watch. "Mr. Benedict asked that we attend a meeting next door in the boardroom at eleven. After that, we'll check with Mrs. Wyse about getting you an office to work from, but for now, please feel free to use mine."

"Thanks. Since there's an hour until the meeting, I'll get started down in the archive room. They have a workstation down there, complete with computer. That's likely the most efficient place for me to begin amassing our list, anyway."

Penelope smiled. Her new admin had used the word "efficient." This was definitely a match made in heaven.

* * * *

"So you think Ms. Martin makes it to the next round?" Alex stood just inside the door to Josh's office.

They only had a few minutes before they had to attend the meeting their dad had called. Josh smiled now, thinking of the breakfast meeting with Andrea. "She definitely made it to the next round. I found her to be clever and attentive." Of course, not quite as clever as Penelope had been, and neither had he felt quite so relaxed at the table as he had yesterday morning.

But then the intimacy he and Alex had shared with pretty Penelope was bound to add shadings of comfort, familiarity, and ease when they were together.

"Good. Well, if you feel positive about her, let's have dinner, the three of us. Say…tomorrow night?"

"I think I'd be more comfortable asking her out for Saturday night, instead. If we call her after the meeting, that should be sufficient advance notice, I think," Josh said.

"Great. How about Sorrento's?" Alex named one of their favorite Italian restaurants.

"Sorrento's will be perfect. Did you reschedule our dinner with luscious Lola?" Josh asked.

"I haven't been able to reach her. But I'll keep trying, and I'll let you know when I do."

"Good. So, do you have any idea why Dad has called this meeting?" Josh had tried to speak to his father privately when he arrived and learned the man was on-site. But his dad had been off, tracking down some of the people he wanted to attend.

"I think it's those letters. He was kind of miffed with us for not mentioning them to him," Alex said.

"Which we didn't do because then he'd likely come to the city, set up camp in the corner office, and give everyone the third degree…kind of like he's doing now," Josh said.

"Yeah, I know."

"The dads need a hobby," Josh said.

"I think we're all agreed on that one," Alex said.

Neither of them said anything else as they made their way to the conference room. The only person Josh was surprised to see there was Penelope. The buff young man sitting next to her seemed to have all her attention.

"Who's that sitting with Penelope?" he asked his brother.

Alex narrowed his eyes as he studied the newcomer. "I think his name is Wildes. From P. A. Communications, I believe."

"Not anymore," Stella said as she maneuvered around them to put pads of paper and pencils in front of each seat. Dad preferred what he called the "tried and true" means of recording thoughts and notes at a meeting, as opposed to the usual tool for that purpose, the BlackBerry.

"What do you mean, not anymore?" Josh asked.

"Since this morning, Andrew Wildes is Ms. Primrose's administrative assistant. I think they make a striking couple, don't you? Of course," she hastened to add, "I'm sure Ms. Primrose is as prim and proper as her name. Still, they do look good together."

Just then Penelope laughed at something her admin said. Josh heard the sound, and it had its usual effect on him, skittering across his skin and settling at the base of his cock. He knew he wore a pissy expression on his face, because that's how he felt. He didn't like the way Wildes was cozying up to Penelope.

And he didn't like the fact that she would laugh like that, all out in public and all, and at something *another* man said.

Stella stopped next to them on her way back to the other end of the table. "I heard they call him 'Wild-man Wildes,' but that's probably just a rumor."

Josh took his seat and continued to stare at Penelope, who as yet hadn't been able to tear her attention away from the "Wild man" to even acknowledge his presence.

Alex sat down next to him and made a grumbling sound that Josh had no trouble understanding.

Just then Penelope looked up. "Oh. Good morning, Mr. Benedict," she said to him. Then she looked at Alex. "And to you, Mr. Benedict."

When she returned her attention to the junior Adonis sitting next to her, Josh turned his head and looked at his brother.

"I think we need to have a word with Ms. Primrose about proper behavior in the office," he said.

"Right after this meeting," Alex agreed.

Joshua would have said more, but just then his father stepped into the room and sent him a steely stare.

Chapter 7

Penelope stole a peek at the two honchos on the other side of the conference table. They didn't look too happy. No, they didn't look too happy at all.

She didn't know what imp possessed her to greet them each so formally after studiously ignoring them from the moment they'd entered the room. Perhaps it was the way they'd left her bed that morning—smug and certain that the *little woman* needed a day to recover from their awesome naked selves before coming into work. Whatever.

Maybe that wasn't what they had been thinking, but it sure had felt that way on her end.

Penelope was beginning to suspect, just from the odd hint she'd picked up here and there, that while the brothers Benedict were indisputably savvy executives—she *had* researched the performance of the company since they'd taken over—and both possessed very high IQs, they weren't terribly knowledgeable when it came to how to relate to women.

Oh, they knew how to make a woman's body sing the "Hallelujah Chorus" and "Ode to Joy," but when it came to dealing with women as sentient, intelligent human beings with whom they needed to interact, they didn't have a clue how to go about it.

She would only be too happy to educate them. She figured she'd best do so as soon as possible, because, against all odds and the uttering of her better angel, she was falling in love with the pair. So educating them would really be to her benefit—and theirs. Otherwise she might bean them over the head with some random blunt instrument.

Penelope sighed. At first she thought she'd write the feelings she had for them off as a residual of the fact that the two of them reminded her so strongly of the men in her dreams, the men who'd so deliciously and sexily haunted her sleep off and on since she'd turned twenty-one. Then she thought, that first night, the way her hormones had reacted and the way the men had been so turned on by *her*, that it had been an aberration, that one in a kajillion happening, to quote Josh.

But looking at them now, she felt that thumping in her heart, that softening of her middle, and she wasn't even particularly aroused. What she was feeling was either the beginnings of a myocardial infarction, or it was love.

Other people entered the boardroom, and their voices produced a low hum. Penelope didn't know why her presence—and the presence of her admin—had been required by Caleb Benedict for this meeting, but he had invited them, and here they were. She'd done her best to put Andrew at ease. He'd confessed that he'd only ever spoken to one of the honchos once, just after he'd started to work at the company. Of course he'd be nervous, being asked to attend an executive meeting.

Caleb stood at the head of the table and said nothing, just waited. When all eyes were on him, he began. "Disturbing letters have been received by the CEOs of this company, over the past month and a half. Letters that have just recently come to my attention."

Penelope hid her smirk, because her lovers both looked chagrined.

"This meeting is to discuss those letters, and to review our security procedures."

Joshua sat forward. "When we received the letters, we handed them over to our security chief, Mitchell Grafton." Joshua nodded at the man who sat on Caleb's right. Then he looked directly at his father. "If we'd thought there had been a need, we would have alerted the family—and you, sir, of course."

"I appreciate your consideration." Caleb's tone sounded dry. Penelope wasn't the only one smiling. "However, now I do know, and at your mother's insistence, here I am. Mitch?"

Mitchell Grafton, whom Penelope had on good authority—Andrew's—was a former Air Force Special Operations commando—got to his feet and pulled out what Penelope presumed to be copies of the letters.

She could see why the man had been a commando. The tall and buff black man gave nothing away in his expression and looked as if he could quite easily eat nails for breakfast. She'd bet he'd been hell on wheels at his job, before taking over as security chief for Benedict Oil and Minerals.

"There were no fingerprints and no DNA found on these letters to give us a clue as to the identity of the person or persons responsible. They were not signed by any known terrorist organization. Indeed, the letters are only vaguely threatening in tone. However, they don't seem to be the usual ranting of your typical environmental whack job—"

Penelope sat up straight. "Excuse me, Mr. Grafton. Is there a difference between an *environmental* whack job and, say, a social or economic or political whack job?"

Mr. Grafton looked right at her. "Um…well, no, Ms. Primrose, I don't suppose there is. A whack job is a whack job."

"Then I would therefore request that you drop the adjective 'environmental' when describing this person."

Penelope noted that several of the people sitting around the table, including her lovers, seemed taken aback by her comments. Caleb Benedict, however, just smiled.

"Penelope has a point, Mitch."

Grafton did give a very slight smile when he nodded to her. "Very well. My point was that this person, whoever he or she may be, seems well educated, and older, as evidenced by the choice of vocabulary used and the faultless grammatical structure employed. This profile raises the level of seriousness with which we should regard these letters."

Penelope thought that conclusion completely logical.

"We're looking at where, exactly, and against whom, precisely, a threat might be carried out," Caleb said. "Again, we have no idea what sort of resources this person might have, which means we have to consider every kind of threat as being viable. Mitch, what's your assessment there?"

Penelope remembered that Grandma Kate had once told her that Caleb had been a Texas Ranger. Retired he may be, but looking at him at the moment, he seemed to her to be every inch a cop.

"Of course." Mitch nodded. "The honchos here are always at the top of any such list—not just because of their being seen by the public as being ultimately responsible for the operation of the company, but also because of their high visibility, being members of the Benedict family."

"We've been down this road before," Alex said. "We are not insensitive to the dangers inherent in our positions and our lifestyles. Josh and I keep our eyes open and our wits about us. This is nothing new, and we refuse, *absolutely refuse*, to alter how we live our lives in the face of any terrorist threat—whether the source is well educated and mature, or not. And I would remind you that our stance is very much in line with family policy. Benedicts don't give in to fearmongers. Period."

Penelope smiled, because she thought that very well said. It was a policy she agreed with wholeheartedly. Anyone who gave in to the possibility of attack by changing their routines, or their habits, handed those who would threaten a victory right then and there.

Mitch carried on as if he'd not been interrupted. "The only other person who rates high on a would-be terrorist's hit list would be the newest member to join our team—Ms. Primrose."

Penelope blinked, and a tremor of shock went through her. "*Me*? Why on earth would I be a target? And I'll remind you I haven't joined your team, Mr. Grafton, I'm employed by—"

"Penelope could be a target?" Josh sat straighter, the insouciant expression on his face gone. In its place was a menacing scowl.

"Explain that," Alex, also scowling, snapped, "right now!"

"An environmental consultant brought in, possibly—and this is public perception we're talking about—to cover up the shameful record of the greedy and evil oil conglomerate—of course she'd be a target. Actually, she's more likely to be the target than either of you two are."

"You'll have guards." Josh shot to his feet, his finger pointing straight at her.

"I most certainly will not!" She got to her feet in response to his decree. How dare he think he could order her around!

"You most certainly will." Alex, also, stood up. He looked over at Mr. Grafton. "I want your best people put on her, twenty-four seven."

"We'll break the armored car out of storage, and make sure you have a driver—"

She didn't give Josh an opportunity to finish. "If you persist in this manner, I will tender my resignation to Mrs. Benedict. And you'll be left to explain *that* to Grandma Kate."

As threats went, that was a good one, Penelope reasoned.

"We'll talk in private after this meeting," Joshua said. "But you will be protected. Not negotiable."

"Damn right we'll talk," Alex said. "And what he just said." Alex pointed at Josh.

"Fine, I'll come to your office," she looked at Alex, "or yours," she said to Josh. "But I'm not changing my mind."

Penelope sat down, well aware that her face was red in anger. She caught a couple of amazed gazes. As her temper cooled—always a very fast process—she wondered if she hadn't been a bit too assertive.

She snuck a glance at Caleb Benedict, who looked pleased as heck. Before she could reason that out, he continued.

"We've decided the best course of action is to slightly upgrade our security, both here and at Benedict Towers. We want department heads to instruct their personnel to be extra aware of their surroundings and to report *anything* that seems even a little off to Mr. Grafton or a member of his team. Do not worry that you're jumping at shadows. If it bothers you, report it."

Amid a flurry of nodding heads, the meeting was adjourned.

"My office. Now." Josh had stood and leaned over the table to deliver that edict.

"Fine."

Both men headed out, not even stopping to talk to their father.

"Do you want me to come with you?" Andrew managed to say that without wincing overmuch. Penelope appreciated the courage it had taken him to make the offer.

"No, thanks. You carry on with compiling that list. Just leave those *honchos* to me."

Once she got the two of them alone, she was definitely going to let them have it.

* * * *

Kate Benedict sat with her legs crossed at the knee. Her mother had tried to break her of that "hoyden-like" habit years before, insisting that a true lady only crossed her legs at the ankle. A smile crossed Kate's lips. Oh, she'd given her mother more fits than most daughters, and never so much so as when she brought home two husbands instead of one.

She missed her Patrick and her Gerald every single day, despite that she'd been without them these past ten years. Some days, she felt every one of her ninety years. On those days, the certain knowledge that before too many more summers passed she'd be with her loves again gave her a unique kind of comfort and strength.

Not that she was a fatalist, she'd never been that. A woman couldn't be married to two men and raise five children without a healthier than average dose of optimism.

She stayed young at heart, primarily by setting goals for herself. Every day she had a reason to get up and get moving. Most of those goals lately had to do with seeing as much of the world as she could, but she still kept an eye on her family, and sometimes it was more than an eye she kept on them.

She would never apologize for wanting her children and grandchildren to be settled and happy. She had been blessed more than most women in life, and truly wanted nothing more than for others to be as fortunate as she had been.

Kate turned from admiring the Houston skyline when the door to the office she was sitting in opened.

"Mother, this is a surprise," Caleb said.

She gave Caleb a big smile. "I thought I'd give you the opportunity to take me to lunch," she said. "Since I was going to do some shopping later anyway. Stella tells me you had called a meeting. What did the boys think of that?"

"Ha. You know, in some ways, my two youngest sons are brilliant. And then there are the other ways."

Kate chuckled. "They remind me so much of your uncles William and Peter."

Caleb frowned. "My bachelor uncles," he said. "They ended up living together and becoming somewhat eccentric, the two of them, didn't they?" He sat down in the chair next to her. "They didn't live to be a ripe old age, either."

"No, they did not. Your grandmother near-to pulled out her hair over them more than once, let me tell you."

"And what did great-grandmother Sarah have to say about them?"

"Sarah was one of the most opinionated women I've ever met. But at the same time, she was quite accepting of however members of her family chose to live, as long as they were happy. Hardly surprising, when you think of it."

Caleb shot her what she could only call a sly grin. "You don't have that last trait in common with her at all, now do you, Mother?"

Kate felt her right eyebrow go up, an automatic kind of reaction when someone challenged her. Or when they outed her. "Of course I do. I'm just also of the opinion that sometimes, young men who take after their eccentric, bachelor great-uncles need a good swift kick in the ass."

Caleb laughed. "Mother, there's no one quite like you in this entire world."

"Thank you. Now, speaking of my grandsons, do you think they're available for lunch?"

"The last I saw of them, they were storming into Josh's office—only a few paces ahead of your Penelope. I don't hear any screaming, but I wouldn't refuse a bet that she's flaying the hides off the both of them even as we speak."

"Well, if not their hides, at least their clothing," Kate murmured sotto voce.

"Pardon?"

Just as well he hadn't caught that. Men—even much loved and otherwise astute sons—could sometimes be dense. Or, following some misguided male-bonding principle, feel the need to stand up for each other when it would be best for them to just keep their noses out of things.

"Nothing, dear." Kate got to her feet. "I think I'm in the mood for sushi."

Caleb winced. "Please, Mother. Not sushi, I beg of you. How about we go chow down on some good old-fashioned Texas barbecue?"

Kate went over to her son and patted his cheek. "Let's compromise. Why don't we go and eat steak?"

"We could go to Spencer's, if that suits?" He got to his feet and headed for the door.

Kate smiled. "Now you're talking. We'll take the limo. While Walter is driving us, you can tell me all about your meeting."

"That's a deal, though there isn't much to tell." Caleb held the door open for her, a simple courtesy, but one she appreciated. "Although Penelope sure has a lot of spunk and isn't afraid to stand up for herself."

"I know," Kate said. "I never would have chosen her otherwise."

"I can't say those are the qualities I'd look for in an environmental consultant," Caleb said.

Kate looked at him for a long moment. "You know, darling, you and Jonathan both need a hobby."

"Believe it or not," Caleb said, "you're not the first person to make just that observation."

Kate laughed, then looped her arm through her son's as they awaited the elevator. "Your Bernice is such a wise woman."

Caleb's expression softened at the mention of his wife's name. *That's just lovely to see after nearly forty years of marriage.*

"She is that," Caleb agreed. "Do you have any ideas on what such a hobby could be? Jonathan and I have been racking our brains, trying to come up with something that sounds appealing."

"As a matter of fact," Kate replied. The elevator bell sounded, and she let her son lead her into the conveyance. She turned and caught sight of the door to Joshua's office just before the elevator doors closed.

She was grateful her sometimes too-observant son didn't see her smile just then. To her, that smile felt positively Machiavellian.

Chapter 8

Penelope's only regret as she stormed into Josh's office was that the door weighed too damn much to make an effective slamming noise when she whipped it shut.

Josh paced while Alex lounged against his brother's desk, hands in his pockets, looking for all the world as if he was so bored by life, he was about to doze off standing up.

She marched right in and started right in. "You listen to me, you two macho honchos. You don't tell me what to do, ever. I don't work for you!"

Alex straightened and Josh spun on his heel. They reached her nearly at the same time.

Pleased with her words and her tone, she finished her mini-rant just as she approached the brothers. Index finger out, she intended to give Josh a sound poke in the chest for good measure.

He grabbed her arms and gave her a good shake instead.

"You're going to drive me crazy, do you know that? If you think for one minute that we'll tolerate *any* threat to you…"

He brought her up and forward and kissed her, his mouth hard on hers, his tongue fierce in its domination of hers.

Penelope's brain told her she should fight this, if only on principle, but once more her body disagreed. The taste of him shot her libido from neutral to full-on arousal in two seconds flat.

Josh's kiss gentled, as if his anger had already evaporated under the heat they made together. He moaned into her mouth, and that sound thrilled her. As soon as he eased his grip of her arms from a grasp to a caress, and slid his hands around her waist, Penelope wrapped her arms around his neck.

Her tongue danced with his, her lips sliding and melding against his mouth as if she'd been starving for the taste of him forever. It felt like days, months, *years* since she'd been held and kissed, instead of the handful of hours she had passed since they'd loved. She pressed her body close, and her nipples peaked as if they recognized the feel of one of her lovers despite the layers of clothing that separated them.

Alex nestled close to them, his hard cock pressing against her hip, his hand stroking her head. "Here. Come here, baby, give me some of your incredible heat," Alex said, and Josh eased back, and then Alex took her in his arms. His kiss differed from his brother's. His mouth, not as hard, not as angry, seemed just as hungry and determined to gobble her down. *Yes,* she wanted to tell him. *I could tell you apart in the dark from just your kisses alone.*

Alex eased away from her much too soon.

"And another thing, pretty Penelope, we don't like you making goggle eyes at your admin like you did this morning during the meeting." Alex's expression looked as serious as she'd ever seen it.

"Dolt," she said the word softly, "I wasn't making goggle eyes at him. I was trying to ease his tension. He's absolutely terrified of anyone whose last name is Benedict."

"Good. He should be." Josh's voice held an edge she'd never heard before.

"No, he should not be. Sheesh." Penelope stepped back from the dynamic duo. Good God, she'd come in to read them the riot act, and in the next breath she tried to tickle their tonsils with her tongue. *That's some compartmentalization I have going on here.*

She walked over to the window, behind Josh's desk, as that was the furthest she could get away from them. She simply couldn't think when they were within such easy reach.

"We have to talk about your tendency to try and tell me what to do as if you were the lords and masters of all your survey." She folded her arms in front of her chest, and nodded her head once to show she meant business. The effect might have been lost, as she had her back to them at the time. She apparently couldn't think too well when she was looking at them, either.

Since she deemed it more important they hear what she said than watch her saying it, she continued to talk and look out at the Houston skyline. "First, this morning you act as if I should just lounge in bed for the day like some weak-willed, simpering little miss and recover from your devastating lovemaking, as if getting up and going to work was beyond my capabilities. And then, in that meeting just now, you go all Neanderthal on me, trying to order my life as if you had the right to do so!" She waited to see if they would respond and heard nothing.

Into the silence came the sound of a lock being engaged.

Penelope whirled around. Josh rounded one corner of his desk while Alex moved toward her from the door he'd just locked, heading for the opposite corner. They clearly intended to get her between them, apparently their favorite place to have her.

"What do you think you're doing?" *Silly question, they're doing exactly what you hoped they would do,* her inner imp whispered gleefully.

"It's lunchtime," Josh said.

"So we're having you for lunch," Alex said.

Oh, goody.

Penelope opened her mouth to make one last attempt to rescue propriety and sense from impending canoodling. Alex drew her forward, and instead, she kissed him.

The taste of them both had become vital to her, a tonic she seemed unable to do without for more than scant minutes at a time. Why did she hunger so for their taste, their touch? What was it about these two men that whenever she was near them, she turned into a raging sex addict?

"I don't understand this." She didn't like the weak sound of her voice but was unable to do anything about it.

"Neither do we, sweetheart." Alex kissed his words down her neck, then down, further, licking and kissing the flesh he bared as he opened each of the buttons on her blouse.

"It keeps getting better and better." Josh's words brushed her ear. He eased her blouse off her then released the hooks on her bra. "So let's stop trying to understand it, and just enjoy it."

Penelope's thoughts scattered when Josh bent down and suckled her nipple. Alex brought his mouth back to hers. His lips slid over hers, wet, erotic, and she could only give herself to the kiss as she felt her passion building, a slow and steady climb.

Her skirt loosened then dropped, and then she felt their hands on her, caressing, petting, seeking her heat, finding her dampness.

Josh ran his fingers up and down the crack of her ass, and Penelope shivered.

"Will you let us take you there later, baby? We'll prepare you. We want to be inside you, both of us at the same time."

"Oh, God." Just the image his words evoked made her shiver. She'd never imagined wanting to feel a man's cock in her ass until now. The thought of having them both inside her at the same time made her knees go weak.

"Yes, I want you both. Oh, my legs." Their heated stroking of her slit, even through her panties, coupled with Josh's sucking on her nipples, took the strength from her legs, and she would have fallen to the floor if they hadn't caught her.

"Here, sweet Penelope. Let us." Josh scooped her into his arms and set her on his desk.

"Lie back, angel," Alex said.

He fastened his mouth on hers again. Their lips mated, back and forth, and then their tongues tangoed, in and out. She feasted on the taste of Alex, loving his kiss, feeding the fire building within her. She reveled in the touch of Josh, whose busy, clever hands kept the flames of her passion burning hotter and then hotter still.

Josh slipped between her legs, eased her panties down and then off. He splayed her legs wide and stroked her hot, wet woman-flesh.

She cried out when she felt his fingers brush her pussy, up and down and then, *yes*, inside her, fucking them in and out of her, driving her wild.

"You're always so wet for us, pretty Penelope."

She heard the sounds that assured her he protected them both. Then she felt the heat of his latex-covered cock, so close. He touched her with it, teasing, and then *in*, finally, all the way inside her, so deep he nudged her cervix.

He stretched her, a miracle. She'd had them a few times now and she thought she'd take them easier, but he filled her and stretched her as if this was their first time, and it felt so good.

"Can you smell us together?" Josh asked.

Alex had moved back but kept his hand on her head, his fingers gently stroking the strands of her pinned-up hair, then down, to brush against her nipples. His gaze seemed riveted on his brother's cock, fucking her.

"Can you smell us together, all of us?" Josh asked again. "The scent of us is pure sexual musk, wild. Erotic." He inhaled deeply, and Penelope moaned, that act somehow seeming rawer, more feral, than any other.

He moved in her, slow, deep thrusts that kept her dangling so close to the precipice, so very nearly *there*. He slid his arms under her legs, and his hands cupped her ass. He increased his pace then, his thrusts hard and fast and deep.

So open, so vulnerable, she was his, could only receive those thrusts and revel in them. Lifting her hips, she tried to rub her clit against the hair that nestled his cock.

Josh chuckled, a dark, thrilling sound. "Mm, you're so hot and good. You need more, baby? You need more of us?"

"Yes, yes!" She begged, and didn't care that she did. She craved, her hands reaching out, grasping as if they could reach the pinnacle, as if she could grab her orgasm and yank it home.

Alex moved closer, took her hand and wrapped it around his cock. "Touch me. Stroke me. Let's come together, this way, this time."

Penelope stroked his cock, urging him closer. When both men understood what she wanted, they moved her, just a little—just enough.

She opened her mouth, took Alex's cock inside it, and relished the heat and the saltiness and that essence that was pure Alex. She'd never loved this the way she did now. Just one more mystery summed up in two words. Why them? Why had she become so turned on by them, when no one else had managed to do so? What was it about them that made it oh, so natural to just let go and feel?

Penelope simply let go of her thoughts, allowed herself to become a woman of sensation, a sensuous woman, a woman who gave and took pleasure. The men groaned and moaned, inhaled sharply and whispered dark, sexy words that drew her even higher. So close, she sucked and swirled and raised her hips, clenching inner muscles and then sucking hard.

"Oh, sweetheart, yes." Alex bent over her slightly and began to rock his hips, his body trembling the way she knew it did when he reached the verge of climax. Josh thrust harder and faster, his hands gripping her ass tighter. Penelope whimpered, needing just that little bit more.

Alex reached down and palmed one breast, pinching her nipple between his thumb and finger, and Josh found her clit and rubbed it fast and lightly, and she went over the edge.

Waves of pleasure washed through her, her own, theirs, in an orgasm so sharp, so sweet, she could only swallow and feel. Thrilling, electric, Penelope wanted to cling to it, to ride it and revel in it and keep it close.

Slowly, oh, so slowly, she came down, came back. Alex eased away from her and then bent down and kissed her, a soft and gentle kiss of thanks.

Josh practically collapsed on her, struggling for breath, but he, too, soon pulled out, carefully. They helped her off the desk and then helped her to dress. Penelope realized that her hair had come down partially.

"Can you fix it?" Alex asked. He looked sheepish, likely because he'd been the one to mess it up.

"Yeah." She used mostly a clip and a few pins and had the knack of fixing her hair down to a science. Then she practically fell onto the sofa. The furniture was deep and comfy. She tilted her head back and closed her eyes and tried to claw back her equilibrium.

"You okay, sweetheart?" Josh sat beside her on her right and picked up her hand. Alex sat on her left and stroked her leg.

"I'm fine. Wonderful. I just wish I could show a little more restraint when I'm around the two of you."

Josh's laugh didn't sound full of humor. "Believe me, you're not the only one. Recent evidence to the contrary, Alex and I are *not* sex maniacs." He paused for a moment, and then said, "You're the first woman we've ever taken here."

Penelope opened her eyes. "I think we need to avoid being alone together in private."

"From now on?" Alex sounded so appalled that Penelope laughed.

"Well, certainly at least during the business day," she said, "while we're here, at the office."

"Agreed." Josh exhaled. "We still don't like the idea you could be in danger because someone has a hard-on for oil companies in general, and ours in particular, at the moment."

"I'm not crazy about that myself. But I agreed with what you said in the meeting. I do believe if you give in to the fear, if you change how you live, how you operate, then you are letting those who threaten, win."

"Damn it." Alex got to his feet. "At least consider some precautionary measures."

"I'm not an unreasonable woman. What kind of measures did you have in mind?"

"Avoid going anywhere alone, for one thing. We have good security here on the premises. I'm going to order Mitch to assign someone to the parking garage at the Towers. It would be difficult for anyone to get in there and mess with your car, but not impossible."

Penelope shivered. She'd never before needed to consider such a horrific prospect. She really couldn't wrap her head around the possibility that she could be a target, just for doing a job. But because her lovers thought it could be so, and they seemed so worried, she'd be as cooperative as possible in order to ease their fears.

"Do you really think I'm in danger? Seriously, this could cause me a lot of grief. I was planning on visiting sites, and doing that soon. I'd wanted to take Andrew with me, because he did work for a school term for the Department of the Interior, and he knows how to take soil and water samples."

She wondered what the brothers were thinking when they looked at each other in just that way.

"About this Andrew 'Wild-man' Wildes," Josh said.

Penelope laughed. She'd only known the young man for a few hours, but the idea that anyone would call Andrew "Wild-man" just seemed totally silly.

When she noticed that both of her lovers stared at her in a way she bet they thought intimidating, she swallowed the rest of her laughter and said, "Yes? What about my admin?"

"What do you know about him, exactly? The two of you looked awfully cozy just before the meeting started. You can't just get all up close and personal with someone you've just met, you know." Josh's earnest expression told her he was quite serious. For his part, Alex nodded his agreement.

Good lord, were they jealous? She'd certainly meant to give these two a bit of a snub earlier as payback for their early-morning attitudes, but she hadn't intended to make them jealous.

"I actually know quite a bit about him, but the most important thing I know is that Stella recommended him for the position as my admin."

She could have gone on to say they were ones to talk about not getting up close and personal on short acquaintance, but figured that would just boomerang back on herself.

Josh and Alex both sighed. The Stella factor seemed to calm them both, considerably.

"Why don't I order up some lunch for us from the restaurant downstairs?" Alex said.

Penelope shook her head. "Let's go downstairs to the restaurant, instead. That way we won't be tempted to indulge in a second helping of booty."

"Good plan," Josh said.

"Speaking of plans, do you have any for tonight?" Alex asked.

"No, I've no plans." Penelope sat straighter, preparing to get up and get moving.

"You do now," Josh said.

"We'll be over at six. We'll bring wine," Alex said.

She could hardly equivocate about their high-handedness when she wanted them to come over. She wanted more of them. This attraction seemed too hot, too fast, to not burn out soon. Until it did, Penelope intended to grab all the heat she could.

She had a feeling that what she shared with Josh and Alex really was a once-in-a-lifetime thing.

"Bring food, too." Penelope headed for the door. "We're going to need to keep up our strength."

Chapter 9

"You've certainly hit the ground running," Caleb Benedict said from the doorway.

Penelope looked up from her desk and grinned, returning the older man's smile. The senior Benedict had just popped his head into her open office.

"Couldn't see any reason not to," she said.

Caleb came into her office and sat in one of the chairs facing her desk. Then, because this was Kate's son, she said, "I need to speak to your mother. I wasn't expecting to be put up in a penthouse apartment, free of charge, nor given a Jaguar to drive. That's way too generous. The salary the Town Trust is paying me is a really good one as it is."

Caleb waved his hand. "It's not as if we went out and purchased those things for you, Penelope. The penthouse is there, anyway, and one of the ones family uses from time to time. It sits empty more often than not. The same with the car. Mother just wanted to be sure you were well looked after. She counted your Gran as one of her best friends. I know she misses her."

Penelope felt a wave of sadness, as she always did when she thought about the passing, earlier that year, of the woman who, for the most part, had raised her.

"I miss her, too. And I think Gran loved her just as much in return. They would stay up chatting until all hours of the morning whenever Grandma Kate came to visit."

Since he *was* here, she said, "Mr. Benedict, I was wondering about something."

"Just call me Caleb," he said congenially.

Penelope nodded. "Caleb, then. I only had a quick look at that map hanging in the boardroom this morning. Could I get another look at it?"

"Of course you can. Come with me. We used to have it hanging in the museum, but then Mother thought it belonged here, so we moved it."

He led her to the conference room they'd used just that morning. The map hung behind the head of the table, the seat Caleb had occupied earlier.

From the glance she'd had of it earlier, she'd thought the map was old. In the bottom corner, the date it had been drawn appeared in fancy script and read *1893*.

"The original Town Trust—that would be Caleb, Joshua, and Sarah Benedict, along with Adam Kendall, Warren Jessop, and Amanda Jessop-Kendall—commissioned the creation of this map. Apparently, shortly after Sarah inherited the estate of Tyrone Maddox, they discovered he'd acquired a lot of land, not just in Texas, but in Arkansas and Missouri, too, speculating on a commodity that at the time wasn't in very high demand—oil."

"Grandma Kate began to tell me stories about your family from the first time I met her, when I first came to live with my Gran when I was ten."

Caleb raised one eyebrow. "Mother doesn't usually share family tales with people she doesn't know that well. And I can't say I've ever heard of her telling the stories to children before."

"I think she wanted to make me feel better, less afraid." Penelope didn't often confide the details of her life. It seemed Josh and Alex weren't the only Benedicts to affect her as no others had. This Benedict had an unusual effect on her, too. He made her feel completely at ease and very loquacious. He felt very—well, *fatherly*. "I'd just traveled across the ocean on my own to live with a grandmother I'd never met. I was ten, as I said, and feeling very afraid and frightened. And angry, you see, because my mother had decided she didn't want me anymore. Kate was there when I arrived—rather unexpectedly, at that. Gran took me in, of course. And Kate told me stories about Sarah Benedict, a young woman who, a century before, had been sold into marriage by her father, to a man who turned out to be a villain. I guess she wanted me to know that life could take a bad turn, yet still turn out for the best in the end."

"That's Mother," Caleb said. He pointed to the map. "Since you do know so much of our family history, I can tell you that while the original Town Trust was trying to decide what to do with some of that land, the use of petroleum oil became more prevalent. So the decision was made to hang on to it, just in case, and to drill that first well." He grinned at her. "A decision we all thank them for."

Penelope understood. While the Benedicts had made their mark as landowners and ranchers when it all began back in the late 1800s, the present day Benedicts could attribute oil as the source of most of their wealth.

"So this is the original family-owned land."

"Yes, all the tracts shaded in yellow belonged to either Benedicts or Jessop-Kendalls."

Penelope looked at the map that depicted Central Texas, stretching up into Oklahoma—although it hadn't been a state when the map had been drawn. It had just become the Oklahoma territory, after having been known as Indian Territory for a number of years.

Words caught her attention, and she moved closer, squinting to get a better look. "It says here, Tahlequah gold deposit, number one." She put her finger under the words. And then she found another notation. "And deposit number two."

"It does," Caleb confirmed.

"There was no gold mined in this area. The geology doesn't favor gold deposits."

Caleb gave her a very slight smile. "It doesn't say gold *mine*. It says gold *deposit*."

She looked from him to the map. "You mean to tell me someone stored gold there?" She double-checked the date on the map. "Why? Owning gold wasn't illegal in this country until nineteen thirty-three."

Caleb said, "Mother didn't tell you the story about Amanda Dupree and what really brought her from Richmond, Virginia to Texas in the first place?"

Penelope searched her memory. "She came to visit her cousin Sarah and ended up falling in love with Adam and Warren, one a Texas Ranger, the other a lawyer, and staying here. Didn't she?"

"Well, certainly. But there was more to the story than that."

Penelope folded her arms across her chest and said, "You're not going to leave it at that, are you?"

"I'll tell you what. Let's go grab a cup of coffee downstairs, and I'll tell you a story about a woman ahead of her time, a famous gunslinger, and some lost Confederate gold."

Penelope grinned. "I could use some coffee right about now."

* * * *

Josh looked up when Alex opened the door to his office. He nodded then got up from behind his desk. This private meeting was taking place later than originally scheduled, in part due to their lunch hour being otherwise so wonderfully occupied.

Thinking about that lunch hour now and the approaching dinner hour that promised to be just as exciting, Josh wanted to rush through this meeting in record time.

He needed to settle himself down. The Legacy Project was an important undertaking, and he needed to give it all due consideration.

His future and the future of his brother, the future of his very *family*, depended upon their making sound decisions now.

"I told Stella on my way in that we didn't want to be disturbed. Do you know she actually smirked at me?"

"It's lowering when she does that," Josh said. "I think the mistake Uncle Carson made was allowing the woman to give us gumdrops when we were kids."

"That could be true. Something about the giving of gumdrops circumvents respect." Alex settled in at the small, round conference table in the corner of his brother's office.

Alex's office was in the opposite corner of the top floor and identically appointed. Truthfully, Josh didn't pay much attention to the furnishings or the decor. When he was working, he generally just focused on the matter at hand.

"We have a meeting with Doug Evercroft tomorrow. I've asked Colt and Ryder to sit in on it with us. That's scheduled for nine a.m., isn't it?" Josh took a seat across from his brother.

"It is, which means our next initial interview for the Legacy Project—my turn—should be the day after tomorrow," Alex said.

"I want to review the entire project to date, if it's all the same to you. I'm afraid a few of the details have slipped my mind in the last couple of days."

"That's fine. I could use a refresher myself." Alex opened the folder he'd brought with him. "Do we need to review the mission statement?" Alex asked.

"No," Josh said. "I think we're clear on that one. We're looking for a wife, a woman who will be the mother of our children, helping to form the next generation of our branch on the Benedict family tree."

"Right. Speaking of family trees, did you know that Penelope seems to know just about *all* our family history?" In Alex's experience, not many people outside the family had much interest in the beginnings of the intertwining of the Benedict, Kendall, and Jessop clans.

"Susan mentioned something to me about that when I called her this morning to explain that we used a few of their…um…provisions. I was surprised, actually. Penelope said Grandma Kate had told her some stories. I just hadn't realized that Grandmother had shared so many details with her. I guess we need to remember that although we've only just met pretty Penelope, Grandma's known her a really long time."

"Did you notice, that first night, at the restaurant? She calls her *Grandma Kate*, too."

"I did notice that." Josh wondered why that felt strange to him. All of his friends, all the years while he'd been growing up, attending school, had called his grandmother Grandma Kate. Josh shook his head, trying to dislodge Penelope from his thoughts.

"Okay, item one." Alex turned his attention to the papers in the folder. "Desirable qualities in a wife. One, must be in possession of a keen intellect. Two, must be open-minded when it comes to matters political and religious."

"That was a good idea you had, insisting the successful candidate not be hot on any particular party or church," Josh complimented.

"I just don't believe in political or religious discrimination," Alex said. "What a person believes should be sacrosanct."

"I agree completely. All right, let's carry on." Josh got more comfortable in his chair.

"Three, must be well established in a career. I was wondering, does that sound, oh, I don't know, snobbish? I mean, really, *career* sounds like we insist the lady have a bunch of initials after her name, and be a top-ranking executive. That's rather…egalitarian of us, isn't it?"

Josh frowned. "Good point. And I don't think that's what we really meant, anyway, was it? Our own mother worked as a sales clerk at Macy's when our dads met her."

"My point, exactly!"

"Why not change number three, then, to read 'Must be meaningfully employed'?"

"Excellent." Alex took a moment to make the correction. "Number four, must have outside interests and accept the same in return."

"We came up with that one during the Thanksgiving Day Cowboys game, didn't we?" Josh said.

"Right after Kelsey dragged Matt and Steven away during halftime at the parents' place and never let them come back for the rest of the game," Alex confirmed.

"I wonder if Penelope likes football?" Josh said. *So much for getting her out of my thoughts.*

"I don't know. We should ask her when we go over there tonight," Alex suggested.

"Yeah, we should. We don't really know all that much about her." Josh felt his mind begin to wander over the lovely, tasty territory that was Penelope Primrose. He hauled his thoughts back to the topic at hand. "Is that all the qualities we came up with?"

"Well, there were others we tossed around, but we decided these four were the most vital. Why? Is something missing?"

Josh said, "Well, a good sense of humor would be nice. And a willingness to, you know, try different things."

"So, what, a sense of humor and a sense of adventure?"

"In the bedroom."

"You want her to laugh at our cocks?"

"No, idiot, a sense of humor in general and a sense of *adventure* in the bedroom."

"Aside from the part where you called me an idiot, I'd say those are both good points. I'll add them." Alex took a moment to jot the last points down. "I have to confess, I have no idea whether luscious Lola has a sense of humor or not," Alex said.

"I have my doubts about Andrea in that area, as well," Josh confessed.

"Well, since we haven't had our second meeting with either lady or told them that they're under consideration for the position of our wife, we could let that one go for the two of them—you know, sort of like a grandfather, um, I mean, grand*mother* clause."

"Did you get a chance to reschedule with luscious, I mean, with Lola?" Josh asked.

"I've called twice, and left a message both times for her to get back to me, but so far, she hasn't returned my call," Alex said.

"Huh. I wonder why not?" Josh sat back in his chair and brought his right knee over his left. "She seemed more than eager when you made the date for the other night, didn't she?"

"She did. When I told her it would the two of us and her, she said she was really looking forward to it."

"How'd she sound when you called and canceled the other night?"

"I explained that Grandmother had unexpectedly arrived. She seemed fine with it." Alex shrugged. "She didn't say anything negative. Just said, 'Fine, thank you for calling.'"

"That's all she said? 'Fine, thank you for calling'?"

"Her very words," Alex said.

"Well, then, maybe it's just a case of her being really busy," Josh said.

"Are you going to call Andrea Martin and arrange to meet her at Sorrento's for the day after tomorrow?" Alex asked. "Since I already made the reservations for three?"

"I've tried once, without mentioning the venue, and left a message for her to call me. You know, now that I think about it, maybe we shouldn't mess with the batting order, as it were. Why not leave another message with Lola and mention we'd like to take her to Sorrento's on Saturday night, but we need to hear from her by Friday evening to make it firm?"

"You're right. We should have dinner with Lola first. I'll call as soon as we're done here."

"Great. Who's next on our list?"

"Our next candidate." Alex flipped to the next page in his folder. "Maria Sanchez, professor of English at Texas State."

Josh smiled. "We can do worse than the lovely Ms. Sanchez, that's for sure. So, who's my next candidate?"

"Ms. Sanchez is the last name on the list."

"We only had three ladies on our list?"

"Three so *far*," Alex corrected. "We haven't been at this for very long. There's the predictable learning curve for us. Don't forget, we haven't even set a project completion date, yet. This is all still in the preliminary stages."

Josh sighed. "That's true." Then he sat back, let his mind go over the entire project, their goals, criteria, progress to date. "I can't help but think we're missing something. That there's some angle or aspect of this we've completely failed to address."

Alex closed the file. "I had a similar sense, just now. Maybe if we let it sit, up here," he tapped his head, "the missing puzzle piece will drop into place."

Josh nodded. "You're right, of course. We're both not only intelligent, we're motivated. The answer is bound to come to us."

"Come to us?" Alex got to his feet, stretched, then lightly bopped Josh on the head with the thin file folder. "Hell, it'll probably march right up and spit in our face and we'll wonder how the hell we ever missed it."

Chapter 10

Why can't I make up my damn mind?

Penelope usually had no difficulty sizing up a situation—any situation—and making a decision. It made no difference if the situation was work related or personal, Penelope never, ever dithered.

Until now.

The brothers Benedict would arrive shortly, for dinner and sex. Penelope took a moment to simply absorb the fact that she now lived in this luxurious penthouse apartment in Houston, Texas. Just outside the glass balcony doors, the city spread out before her clear to the horizon. As the sun began to set, the lights of Houston started to blink on, like a carpet of thousands of dazzling jewels to tempt the imagination.

Situated in the perfect place to enjoy this panoramic view, the dining room rectangular table awaited her pleasure.

She couldn't decide whether to give the table a romantic kind of setting, or not. Would Josh and Alex think it, and therefore she, was hokey? Would they worry she was trying to be too romantic?

Was she being too romantic?

There had been no promises spoken or implied between them—unless you counted their apparent jealousy of her administrative assistant earlier that day. They'd had sex on three separate occasions, but they hadn't gone out anywhere, like on a date. So what was this thing happening between them, anyway?

She couldn't really count eating in the same restaurant on the day she met them as a date, because that had evolved from the meeting of the Lusty, Texas Town Trust. After the meeting, the impromptu family-style celebration had just kind of happened at *Lusty Appetites*. She'd been carried along with the crowd, as it were. Besides, she hadn't even *sat* with the men.

Decisions, decisions.

So did she set the table, using the dramatic backdrop of the glistening Houston night scene and the Benedicts' finest china, silver, crystal, and candles, creating a nice romantic ambiance? Or did she just toss some paper plates on the table, along with a roll of paper towels, and call it done?

Penelope couldn't make up her mind.

In a flash of insight, she realized the matter before her wasn't really about the dinner table at all. The real question was, did she want to try and edge this relationship from the purely physical toward something more on the path to the permanent, or just keep it as a temporary, intermittent booty-call arrangement?

Penelope hadn't come to Texas to look for love. She came to do a job, to live someplace different. She came to get away from all the familiar places where she was faced with constant reminders of the grandmother she'd so recently lost. She came to give herself space and a chance to figure out what she wanted to do with the rest of her life.

She realized after her grandmother's funeral that, in a way, she'd been living her life as if everything about it had been temporary. Though she'd not understood it at the time, her mother's rejection had scarred her deeply. At ten, she'd only just begun to wonder what her father might have been like. He'd died before she'd been born, and he'd had no family. She hadn't been the only fatherless child in her area of London wondering just that very thing. But when she'd come home from school that day to be faced with her mother, expression rigid, with an old, secondhand suitcase in hand, and told she was going to live with her grandmother in America, something inside her had shattered.

Penelope blinked. The lights of Houston had blurred. She wiped her tears, angry with herself for allowing maudlin emotion to swamp her. Allowing *that person* to upset her anew.

To hell with it.

She'd lived her life eating off paper plates—metaphorically, if not literally. She was worth the good china.

Damn right I am.

It didn't take Penelope long to set the table. To make it seem less formal, she decided against using a tablecloth. Instead, she'd selected three black, rectangular place mats. The plates gleamed now in the candlelight, pretty white with a gold rim and tiny yellow roses in a cluster. The china looked as if it had barely ever been used. Next she'd set out glasses, two for each of them, a water goblet and a wineglass. She liked wine, but she also had gotten in the habit of drinking water with her meals. The stainless steel cutlery wasn't silver, but that was just as well. She didn't have to polish the stainless.

An array of linen napkins had awaited her selection. She chose the ones that were the same rich yellow as the roses on the china. There even was a selection of napkin rings. She picked the green ones. Finally, two crystal candlesticks with tapered white candles finished the effect. Whoever had arranged the buffet's drawers had thoughtfully provided a candle lighter.

Penelope had set flame to the candles then stood back and eyed the table critically. It looked nice. Penelope smiled. It did look nice, and maybe that was all the justification she needed for the fuss.

The doorbell rang.

She looked down at herself as she went to the door. The camisole and capris she'd put on after her shower were comfortable and attractive. *I won't likely have them on for long anyway, so it hardly matters.*

She checked the security viewer, then opened the door.

Josh and Alex came in, each giving her a quick kiss first. Alex carried a large, white paper bag, and Josh's hands were full carrying a bottle of wine each.

"I thought we'd eat in the dining room."

"Good idea," Josh said. The men headed directly there. Penelope followed, anxious to see their reactions to her table-setting efforts.

"We'll need a corkscrew. I'll get it," Josh said. He set the bottles on the table then headed to the kitchen.

"Can I help?" she asked as Alex began to set out the round, sealed containers that had been in the bag. The food, whatever it was, smelled delicious.

"We need four serving spoons." He looked up and smiled. "And wise of you to give us each two glasses. May I suggest a pitcher of ice water?"

"Am I going to need it?" she asked, half joking.

"You might," Josh said as he came back into the dining room. He made quick work of opening the first bottle of wine, something red. "Since you'd never tried salsa on your eggs, we thought that perhaps you should have an introduction to Tex-Mex cuisine."

"Oh, good! I wouldn't have known what to try on my own. I do have a sense of adventure, but sometimes that trait can land you in such muck. Just let me get the water."

Penelope wondered about the strange look the brothers exchanged, and then she let it go. If she worried about every odd look or comment, she'd get herself into a state of antacid dependency in no time flat.

She came back into the dining room carrying a crystal pitcher of ice water and poured some for each of them.

Josh and Alex each had a hand on her chair, and together saw her seated so that she faced the beautiful view. With a man on both ends of the table—close enough she could link fingers—she set her napkin on her lap and prepared to sample a new, to her, cuisine.

Josh poured wine into everyone's glass as Alex pried the lids off the containers. Both men then set about scooping the steaming hot contents onto their plates, and hers.

"You've got Mexican rice, chili, chicken taco—a soft taco, this first time out—and our all-time favorite, spicy beef tamales."

They both seemed so pleased with themselves that Penelope had to smile. It did all smell very appetizing. She forked a bit of rice. The flavor exploded onto her tongue, garlic and cumin and chili peppers.

"Oh, that's good." She gave them each a smile. "I love rice."

The chili she recognized, of course, and carefully sampled it, relieved when it didn't set fire to her tongue. Since comments seemed to be expected, she said, "Mmm."

Penelope had no idea what to do with the long yellow thing on her plate that looked as if it was tied with a ribbon.

It didn't seem to be leaking anything. Was this one of those foods one ate with their fingers?

She picked it up, and turned it first one way, and then the other. "Which end do I bite into first?"

"No! You open it and eat what's inside." Josh only smirked a little.

"Oh, of course." She watched the men, then copied their actions. Once she saw what was inside, she looked up at Alex. "This didn't come off a sidewalk somewhere? Because if I saw that on a sidewalk, I'd go around it."

"No, sweetheart. It's beef and spices and…stuff. It's good. Try it." His voice sounded funny.

"Are you laughing at me?"

"Only a little, honest," Alex answered for the both of them, primarily because it seemed Josh was having some sort of breathing problem and couldn't speak right then.

"Maybe I'll serve you the grand English dish, toad in the hole, and see what your face looks like."

"As long as the toad is deceased, I'm game," Josh said.

Penelope laughed and, because they were being so sweet, dared to try the interesting-looking filling from the tamale.

"Oh! It's yummy!" Actually, the tamale turned out to be her favorite. She did need more than a sip of water, but by the time she'd finished, she thought she'd developed a taste for the spicy Tex-Mex cuisine—at least as much of it as she'd sampled.

"So the next time I scramble some eggs for you, I can cover them in hot salsa?" Josh asked.

"Um…perhaps in a little bowl on the side?" She didn't want to tell them the idea of salsa on eggs for breakfast didn't sound particularly appealing.

Judging by the smiles they gave her, she guessed they figured that one out on their own.

They worked well together, and cleanup didn't take long. They moved back into the dining room, drawn back to the beautiful sparkling lights outside the window.

"Have you tried the Jacuzzi out yet?" Josh poured the last of the wine into their glasses.

Penelope savored one more sip of the merlot and then set her glass down. "No. I was waiting for the two of you."

"Were you, now?" Alex set his glass down and came over to her. He cupped her face in his hands and kissed her, his lips light and moist against hers. Reaching up, she grasped his wrists, held on to him. She felt the strength of his pulse, inhaled the scent of him, an aroma familiar and arousing. Inside, her heart began to beat just a bit faster as tiny tendrils of arousal swam through her blood.

"I think you're turning me into a sex addict." She whispered those words against Alex's mouth, and then turned her head so she could kiss Joshua.

Honeyed and hot, his flavor sank into her, became a part of her. Together, they made a heady and perhaps dangerous combination. The taste of one followed by a sip from the other heated her blood and stirred her juices like nothing else on earth.

"You can only be a sex addict if you're a celebrity who's gotten caught cheating." Alex grinned as he said that.

"So if I'm not a sex addict, what am I?"

"Delectable and delicious," Alex said.

"Sexy and seductive," Joshua said.

"You're also overdressed." Alex pulled the camisole over her head, and then Josh unhooked her bra. Both garments hit the floor.

Alex picked her up, so she wrapped her arms around his neck and kissed him, her tongue sweeping his mouth, eager to drink as much of him as she could. She sensed Josh's hands on her waist, and then felt him peeling her capris and panties down her legs and off her. The moment her feet were free of the clothing, she wrapped her legs around Alex's waist.

"Now who's overdressed?" she whispered against his neck.

Alex chuckled. "We are, sweetheart. But we'll fix that as soon as we get into the bathroom."

"Hurry."

Penelope trusted Alex not to drop her, even when she nibbled and licked his neck and his cock hardened beneath his jeans in response. Joshua must have gone ahead of them because the moment Alex carried her into the master bedroom she heard the sound of the Jacuzzi jets.

"Here, sweetheart. You get in, and we'll be with you in just a bit." Alex lowered her into the water.

Penelope sighed. The heat and bubbles felt wonderful. She moved to the other side of the large tub. Relaxing, she got comfortable, preparing to watch the men strip for her.

Josh began to take his clothes off, but Alex left the room. He was back moments later with a small plastic bag.

"What do you have there?"

Instead of answering her, he withdrew the items and held them up for her to see.

"You'll have to tell me what they are. Until the two of you came into my life—pun definitely intended—my sexual experience and knowledge were miniscule."

Josh grinned. "Corrupted you, have we?"

"Considerably." She couldn't say that with a straight face. "That wasn't a complaint, by the way. It was only an observation."

"I know." Josh finished undressing and eased into the tub. He came to her and kissed her lightly. "We bought some lube and a butt plug. We want to be inside you at the same time, pretty Penelope. To do that, we have to prepare your ass to receive cock. This will also give you a chance to see if you'll enjoy anal play, or not."

Penelope looked over at Alex. He'd set the two items on the shelf above the tub and then began to undress.

"It's your decision," Alex said. "We hope you'll say yes and that you'll like it."

"So what will it be, sweetheart?" Josh's question tickled her belly, the deep sound of his voice an indication of his arousal.

"I never imagined I'd have such a sense of adventure when it came to sex." Just thinking about having both of these men inside her at the same time made her horny as hell. They were just so damn sexy, the both of them. Especially when they looked at her the way they were doing now, waiting for her answer.

"Yes. I want you both inside me at the same time. I want you every single—and double—way I can have you."

Chapter 11

Penelope reached up and removed the clip holding up her hair, and then gently shook her head, releasing those lustrous midnight tresses to cascade down her body.

That sensual act stopped Alex in his tracks, with his shirt off and pants just open. Some of her hair floated on the water, and he saw again that apparition from his long-ago dreams. When those visions would haunt his sleep, he'd believed he was watching Aphrodite, the goddess of love, in a private moment as she bathed, and then beckoned to a lover.

Now he wondered if that had been the right interpretation at all. Because right here, beckoning to him with that coy smile, awaited his very own personal Aphrodite. Then she raised her arms to him, and he melted.

"You're a miracle." The words escaped unplanned, but he wouldn't regret them. She *was* a miracle—to be so turned on by both him and Josh, to be responsive to them both, willing to share her body with them so generously.

"No, Alex. I'm only a woman."

Alex shucked the rest of his clothes then eased into the spa. Josh sat back, spread his arms out along the edge of the tub, and smiled. His brother must have realized how triggered he was. Alex appreciated the gesture because he couldn't wait to get his hands on Penelope.

Alex knew that Josh would content himself, for the moment, to watch. Alex would return the favor next time.

They'd shared a few women over the years, enough to have convinced them both that they wanted to share *the* woman one day, to form the same kind of family they were raised in. He and Josh were connected in the same way he believed Matt and Steven were, the same as his own fathers were. They always had been, even as kids, long before the thought of females and sex had ever entered their heads. He'd always believed that he'd never feel as close to another person as he did to his brother Joshua.

Now he understood he'd been wrong.

Alex let his thoughts slip away and focused on Penelope. Her delicious self, wet and naked, was his for the taking. "No, you're more than just a woman. You're arousing, and electrifying. You blow me apart and put me back together again, and you make me hunger for more of you. All of you."

"Then take all of me." She closed the distance between them. Wrapping her arms around him, she pressed her body close to his.

He could feel the pebbled points of her nipples pressing against his chest. Her skin, so soft, so silky, heated beneath the caress of his hands. He lowered his mouth to hers, breathed her in, and then kissed her.

Her flavor, like honeyed wine, rich and intoxicating, flooded him. The taste of her stroked him to a fine arousal, quenched his thirst and parched him in the same sip. He needed to taste more of her, and then still more. How did she do this to him? No other woman ever had.

He used his tongue to drink from her, to touch and taste every bit of her mouth. When he played his hand down her back to her gorgeous ass, she sucked his tongue, stroking it, and the action was the same as she'd used on his cock.

That organ stiffened and bobbed as if it could capture her attention and her mouth.

While keeping her mouth on his, she fisted him and stroked him with a touch both firm and deep.

He ended the kiss. "You get me so hot, so fast. A part of me wants to just splay you wide and plunder."

The sound she made told him more than words could have the idea appealed. "I won't break." Her murmur bathed his face as she placed tiny little kisses all over him.

Alex shivered in response to her offer, the kind of offer every man, if he's honest with himself, longs to hear.

Those three words were saying take me, do as you will with me, no holds barred. It was the most generous offer he'd ever received.

"I know you won't break." He caressed her face. "But I might."

Penelope's laugh, so damn female and sexy, skittered across his dick then settled deep inside of him.

He eased her back so he could bend down and suckle her nipples. She loved her breasts being played with, loved the strong suction he gave her. When she arched, he stood and brought her to the other side of the tub. "Can you reach the condoms?" he asked her.

"Yes."

He let her slide down his body so she could put the rubber on him. Then he sat and brought her over his lap so that she straddled him. He looked over her shoulder at his brother, who nodded. Josh slid over to retrieve the lube and the butt plug.

Alex turned his attention back to Penelope. His cock pulsed from the nearness of her, from the heat of her pussy pressed against him. It really did take every bit of effort not to just plunge and take. But he wanted to pleasure her, to get her ready for what would come next. "Let's see how high we can make you soar."

* * * *

Penelope closed her eyes to better savor the amazing sensations coursing through her. Head back, she arched her spine, pressing her breast closer to Alex's incredibly talented mouth. At the same time, she undulated her hips, rubbing her pussy against his hot, hard, latex-covered cock. Her labia spread, and his erection nestled between them, a yummy feeling.

Water rippled around her. She felt the heat of Josh's body as he joined them, as he came up behind her and pressed his naked body against her back. He cupped the back of her head and turned her just a little. His hot, moist breath caressed her lips, and then his mouth settled on hers.

How amazing to kiss one lover while being pleasured by another. She used her tongue to taste and tease, to drink his essence in as she had his brother's. Why did the taste of these two men excite her, when no other kiss had been more than just nice?

All of her thoughts scattered when Josh's lips left hers to trail sweet kisses and arousing nips down her cheek, her neck, and then around to her shoulder.

"Take me inside, sweetheart." Alex's plea vibrated against her breast. *Yes.* She rose up and used her left hand to place his cock at the opening to her cunt. Then slowly, savoring every inch of him, she lowered herself onto him.

He pulsed inside her, one heavy spasm in greeting, and she squeezed him in response, her body's welcome a tiny shower of her juices to coat his cock.

"You're so hot and tight around me. I love being inside you."

"Mmm." Focusing on the sensation of his cock moving within her as she raised and lowered herself again and again, words seemed impossible. So she used another form of communication, and captured his mouth with hers. His tongue immediately began to thrust in and out of her mouth, arousing her even more. To have him inside her twice felt like heaven.

"You look so damn sexy riding him." Josh's words whispered in her ear, his breath tickling her there, making her shiver.

"While you're fucking him, I'm going to play with your ass, baby." The words sounded dark and dangerous, thrilling her.

"Oh, yes, please." She wanted so much to take everything they gave her, to see what new delights existed that she'd never tasted before.

"Cold."

The word of warning touched her just a moment before the cold sensation against her anus. The combination of the chilled and silky gel and the heat and caress of Josh's finger as he smoothed the lube up and down, coating the outside of her tiny rosette, made her moan in pleasure.

"Oh, yes." She'd never been touched like that, and the arousal it caused made her clench her pussy.

"She likes that," Alex said.

"More now, baby."

Before she could ask him more what, he smoothed a fresh coating of the lube on her, and then on the downward stroke across her anus, he centered on the opening and began to push.

Penelope gasped as the pressure built, as it stung just a little. Then she felt herself opening slowly and Josh's finger penetrating her.

"Oh!" Tiny little quivers ran through her. The feeling distracted her, and she stopped moving on Alex.

Alex put his hands on her waist and began to move her up and down on his cock at the same time he leaned forward to capture her nipple again.

Josh moved his finger in and out of her ass, his pace slow and measured. Penelope groaned. She couldn't help it. It felt as if some nerve ending ran from her ass to her nipple, and then all the way down to her clit. She shivered, rested her forehead on Alex's, and resumed riding him. She wanted to rush, but he controlled her, keeping her to his pace, and though it thrilled her, she realized he kept her to *his* pleasure. That realization only made her burn hotter.

"More."

Josh's one word made her pelvic floor muscles contract. Her body, awakened and needy, seemed to have a mind of its own as she pushed down on Alex and then out toward Josh at the same time.

"Why, pretty Penelope, does your ass want another finger?"

"Please." This was different than anything she'd ever experienced. New, exciting, more, Penelope wanted all she could get of it. "I want to come."

"Not yet, baby," Alex said, and she understood then just how well the two brothers knew each other.

Josh stood close enough that the heat from his body blanketed her. Then he edged closer, more to the side, his head lowered so that his words tickled her ear. "Does it feel good, pretty Penelope?" he asked as he fucked his fingers in and out of her.

She knew he looked over her shoulder, that he could see his brother's cock moving in and out of her.

"It feels so good…oh, please…I need *more*." How liberating to beg freely, to expose this side of herself, this raw, physical side.

"What you need is Josh's cock in your mouth," Alex said. "Suck him, sweetheart."

A creature now of pure sexual desire, Penelope turned her head, bent down, and took Josh's cock into her mouth. She felt his fingers comb into her hair, then hold her head firmly even as he began to thrust into her.

The taste of Josh's cock fed the need in her to give, to let loose and be just here, with them, steeped in every pleasure under the sun, taking, giving. Here, now, this was all that mattered. This was everything, and Penelope rejoiced as her ardor began the upward spiral, courting release.

"That's it, sweetheart, suck him." Alex's words spurred her on to give more. The hand on her head now was his. She moved up and down on one cock, sucked in and out on the other in complete libidinous abandon.

"You have such a fucking great mouth." Josh's fingers had stilled in her ass, his head rested just above her own, and she felt the tremors he couldn't control.

Then his fingers left her, but before she could even think to complain, he moved slightly, and she felt something else, something harder and larger press against her anus.

And then Josh said, "Now."

Alex reached down and stroked her clit, his movements light and fast. Her orgasm burst out of her, hot, wild, and exciting. She nearly screamed as the sharp pleasure knifed through her, and would have, but Josh's cock twitched in her mouth. She drew on it deeply, coaxing his seed from him.

The pressure against her anus increased, and then she felt the butt plug slide into place. Her climax peaked again, and Penelope shivered in bliss even as she swallowed Josh's seed.

Alex grabbed her hips and held himself deep inside her. She felt his cock pulsing inside her as he came.

"Holy hell." Josh eased his flaccid cock from her mouth and leaned on her for a few moments, stroking her back as he fought for breath.

Penelope relaxed against Alex, eyes closed, and let appreciation for the orgasm settle into her thoughts. She didn't want to move, she just wanted to lay against one lover with the other close by and *be*. The sensation of having that butt plug inside her kept her arousal there, kept it at a tiny quiver.

"Come here, sweetheart, and let Alex clean up." Josh lifted her, and she opened her eyes. He sat on the bench in the tub and cradled her on his lap.

The water still bubbled around them, still warm. Lassitude crawled through her, and she yawned.

"How does that feel inside you?" Josh asked.

"Different. It's kind of keeping me horny, but just a little."

"We won't leave it in very long, this first time. Just until we go to bed."

"Probably not good to stay in the tub too long, either." Penelope had only enjoyed a hot tub a few times in her life, and had always considered it a luxury.

She could easily get used to it.

"It can be a problem, but because we Benedicts tend to, um, use this facility for more than just soaking in, we set them at just a hundred degrees. One hundred and four is the highest any tub should ever be set at, and in fact none of our spas will go above that temperature."

Penelope kept her eyes closed, with her head on Josh's shoulder. She couldn't hold back her smile. Trust Josh to have the facts and figures close at hand.

The water swirled as Alex sat down beside them. He kissed Penelope's shoulder. "Will you let us stay tonight?"

They hadn't slept apart since they'd met. She liked that they didn't take for granted that they could just stay.

"Yes, please. I like sleeping between the two of you."

"When we've let you sleep."

Josh's low, gentle words found her opening her eyes. She caressed his face, and then Alex's. "I'm not complaining."

"Like I said, you're a miracle." Alex placed another kiss on her shoulder, then got out of the tub. He dried himself quickly, then grabbed a fresh towel and held it out toward her. "Come on, Penelope, let's get you dried off and tucked in between us, then."

Josh lifted her over the edge of the tub, and Alex took her into his arms. Penelope let the men take care of her.

A woman could get used to this. She just wasn't certain if getting used to this kind of pampering was a good idea.

Because if they ever stopped, if it ever ended, she might never get over it—or them.

Chapter 12

Penelope rubbed her hands together in glee. It was finally time to go out in the field and get to work.

She didn't spout facts and figures at the drop of a hat the way Josh did. Neither did she sit and form long, drawn-out analyses the way she suspected Alex did. However, she knew in her heart she was just as much of a nerd as her men were.

Penelope froze, her hand extended to pick up a file. *Her men.* She'd best get that thought right out of her head. Good grief, they hadn't even taken her out to dinner! They weren't "her men." She had no claim on them. Yes, they'd been pretty damn intimate, and could barely keep their hands off her. For that matter, she couldn't keep hers off them, either.

That didn't mean anything more than what it was. Essentially, they were friends with benefits.

Penelope sighed. She wasn't going to feel guilty about that. She figured it really was a one in a kajillion chance for her to react to even one man the way she had, let alone two. Based on her brief experience before meeting the brothers Benedict, she would have stated with absolute conviction she wasn't a touchy-feely or a passionate woman.

She still didn't think she was—except with them. For all she knew, this heat, this fire, would die down as suddenly as it had erupted. So while she could, and while it lasted, she wasn't going to overanalyze it, she was just going to enjoy it.

Which meant she needed to stop thinking of Josh and Alex as her men.

Penelope mentally shoved the Benedicts into their compartment and picked up the first folder on the stack that her able admin had placed on her desk.

She scanned, sorted, and thought about the wide spectrum of drill and mine sites, especially the ones which had been remediated.

Andrew came in bearing two take-out cups of coffee.

"Thanks." She took the one he offered and set it down.

"You're welcome."

"What's put that stunned expression on your face?" Penelope thought he looked as if he'd seen a ghost.

"I just met Mrs. Benedict. Mrs. *Katherine* Benedict."

His awed tone made Penelope want to giggle, but she resisted the urge because she didn't want to hurt his feelings. To her, the woman in question had always been the nice lady who'd been with her grandmother the day she'd arrived. She could understand how, for someone who worked for the Benedicts, and who listened to Texas lore, Grandma Kate would achieve near rock-star status.

Before she could think of something to say, he said, "She knew my name!"

"She's a very nice woman," Penelope said. "I've known her since I was little, because she was a friend of my grandmother's."

"But how would she know my name? I'm just a nobody."

"Andrew, you are not a nobody!" Penelope hated when people thought of themselves that way.

"Up until a few days ago, I was just an accounting clerk—a drone in a company that employs thousands of people."

"Is that how this company makes you feel? Like you're just a drone?" Penelope's first employer had been that way, and it wasn't a tenth of the size of Benedict Oil and Minerals. She knew very well how it felt to be nothing more than a faceless, nameless entity. She really hoped that wasn't how the Benedicts did business. Yes, the bottom line was the bottom line. But instilling a sense of worth in those who worked for you didn't require money. It just required heart.

She brought her attention back to the moment and noticed that Andrew looked uncomfortable. "No, of course they don't. That wasn't a criticism of the management here, honest. It was just a statement of fact. There are thousands of people employed, directly or indirectly, by the Benedict family. It amazed me the matriarch would know who I am, that's all." He looked down at his feet, then back up at her. "Actually, this is my third employer, and by far the best. I'm going to do everything in my power to stay here as long as I can."

Penelope wanted to ease his embarrassment. "Likely, Mrs. Benedict knew who you were because Stella Wyse recommended you for this position. From what I can gather, the two women are good friends."

"Huh." Andrew ducked his head. "I'm afraid I stumbled all over my words when she asked me how I was doing. I hope she doesn't think I'm an idiot."

"I'm sure she doesn't." Penelope motioned for her admin to sit down. Then she nodded to the files. "Good job on gathering so much information so quickly. I thought we'd start with the sites reported as being remediated. They should take the least amount of our time. We'll likely head out right after lunch to the first one, just this side of Brady. It'll take us more than a couple of hours to get there. We likely won't get back until late, though. I'm thinking around six-thirty or seven."

Andrew looked at his watch. "Mrs. Wyse mentioned the supplies you ordered arrived this morning. They're being stored down in the general supply room. Do you want me to grab the water and soil test kits?"

"I'd actually like all the test kits and instruments brought up here, so they're on hand. While you do that, I'll print us up a map and some charts I've designed to use at each site. I thought we'd each take notes, then compare when we come in from the field."

"Yes, ma'am."

Penelope blinked when he called her ma'am. She wasn't even two years older than he was! Having never been anyone's boss before, she realized she'd have to work on getting used to it.

"I'll go get them now." Andrew paused at the open door and looked out into the reception area.

Penelope smiled because she realized he was checking to see if Grandma Kate was still visible. Then he sighed and left.

She turned back to her computer and downloaded the charts and graphs she'd designed herself. Selecting the ones she needed, she began printing them off. This would be her first real day in Texas doing the work she believed in, the work she loved to do.

She couldn't wait to get out in the field and get started.

* * * *

"I know there's a lot of oil there," Douglas Evercroft said. "The geology supports it, and my surveyors assure me that it's a site that will prove very lucrative." He sat back and puffed out a breath. "Wanting my money all up front may seem extreme, but compared to the money you'll make with all those barrels of good Texas oil, you'll feel like you stole it."

Josh grinned. He had to give Evercroft credit. The man certainly did his best to come out on top, no matter what.

They'd been negotiating off and on for several weeks and through that time had been haggling over the price of the land and the terms of payment.

"Since you're convinced we'll all be swimming in crude, you shouldn't mind that we pay half the agreed upon price up front, and turn the rest into a percentage of the barrels pumped *as* the oil is extracted."

Doug returned Josh's smile. "Now, son. I've been around the block a time or two. Back when your Uncle Carson was just getting a feel for that chair you're sitting in now, I knew how things worked in this town. Hell, I started out as a roughneck, worked my way up from nothing. I've scrubbed my share of crude out from under my fingernails, that's a fact. There's nothing to stop you from making that deal with me and then letting the site go to reserve. The oil don't get pumped, I don't get paid. Especially now that you've got that fancy environmentalist from back east sniffing all around. Likely you'll be putting a lot of stuff on hold till she goes back to Washington."

Josh sat back and studied the man for a moment. One thing he'd been able to count on all his life, aside from his brother, were his instincts. Right now they were screaming at him. It rattled him to have thoughts of Penelope brought to the table, as it were.

"I don't know where you got your information, Mr. Evercroft." Josh sure as hell didn't like that he had it, either. He looked over at Alex and saw his brother looked as surprised as he felt. Then he noticed that both Colt Evans and Ryder Magee had sat up straighter in their seats, focusing on Evercroft.

There'd been no progress tracing those letters, and the fact that Penelope could be a target worried him more each day. For Evercroft to even know about her, it meant someone here had leaked information to the man. Was it connected to their threat? Josh didn't know—and he didn't like that he didn't know.

"The family has hired a consultant, that's true. In light of recent events, we want to be absolutely certain that all remediated sites have been properly rehabilitated."

He sat back and looked at his brother.

Alex leaned forward. "We have no problem whatsoever adding a clause to the contract that will allow for stiff penalties on our part if we don't develop the site according to a timeline we can all agree upon."

Evercroft winced, as if he really didn't like the sound of those terms. "I don't know. A man's got to protect himself in this day and age. Paying me the money once we sign just seems like the straight-up way to do things."

Josh looked at him for a long moment, until the man blinked. "Are you doubting the veracity of a contract signed with Benedict Oil and Minerals—or the report of your own geologists? Perhaps you're worried there isn't as much oil there as you'd like us to believe."

"Your company's always been rock solid." Evercroft looked like a man who'd just lost a pissing match. "And hell, you know these scientists are right most of the time."

"Then we'll have our lawyers include a provision for penalties if we fail to drill," Alex said. "We'll pay you half of our previously agreed upon price up front, and the rest as a percentage of the production, as the oil is pumped from the ground."

For a long moment, Evercroft said nothing. He just sat there, staring at his fingers as they tapped out a beat on the table. Finally, slowly, he nodded.

"Well, then. You have your legal eagles write everything up, and send it over to my boys." Then he smiled. "You can understand my concerns. Once I heard you had an environmentalist sniffing around, I began to worry. These are difficult times for the oil industry."

"I'd be interested in knowing how you heard about Ms. Primrose." Colt spoke up for the first time, his tone full of good-old-boy humor. "Since Ryder and I only just found out, ourselves, and we're practically family."

"Oh, you know how this town is, boys. They say women gossip, but swear to God, men have that habit down to a fine art form."

Josh wanted to press the issue but knew they were better off letting it seem an incidental matter that he'd known about Penelope. He thought he did a passable job of winding up the meeting as if the matter was already forgotten and showing Evercroft to the elevators.

When he returned to the boardroom, Alex said, "Mitch is on his way up."

"You want to kick something, there, Josh?" Ryder asked. "You look a mite pissed."

"Son of a bitch." Josh paced to his window. "It's likely not connected to those letters. Still—"

"There's a threat to your woman. Trust me, Ryder and I both know how you feel about that," Colt said.

Josh spun on his heel as Colt's words registered. He opened his mouth to protest, then shut it again. He hadn't thought of Penelope as being *their* woman. Looking over at Alex, he could see his brother had reacted the same way. That's the second shock in just a few minutes. Josh really did not like being taken by surprise this way. He and Alex would have to talk about this. But later. Since it seemed as if Colt was waiting for some kind of response, he said, "Grandma Kate's fond of her. So of course we wouldn't want anything to happen to her."

He couldn't interpret the look the wildcatters exchanged between them. Until Ryder said, "You keep on telling yourself that for as long as you need to, Josh. We understand completely."

Well, hell. Josh shook his head. He'd let that one go, mainly because Ryder had a point. He and Alex had been studiously *not* thinking about their relationship with pretty Penelope since the first time they both slid into her hot, delectable body. He needed to get Penelope out of his thoughts. Thank God he was standing behind a chair. No one would know he had a hard-on.

"Perhaps we can ask Mitch about having someone from security accompany Penelope this afternoon," Alex said.

"Accompany her? Where the hell is she going?" And why hadn't Josh known she was going somewhere? He was the oldest, damn it.

That thought, and what it meant, echoed in his brain until he pushed it away.

"She's heading out to the number four site, just outside of Brady," Alex said. "I only just found out before our meeting, and only then by accident. I overheard her admin talking to Stella."

"Damn right Mitch will have someone go with her." Josh glared over at the wildcatters, both of whom seemed to have come down with a coughing fit. He supposed he should get used to the fact that he had two new brothers who felt perfectly comfortable razzing him the way brothers did.

So the best thing Josh could do was ignore them. He had a feeling he was going to need all his energy keeping his worry for Penelope under wraps until she got safely home again.

Chapter 13

Home at last.

Penelope sighed when she got out of her car at Benedict Towers. The security guard on duty looked to be about as easygoing and fun-loving as Mitch Grafton had been.

She was going to give those two Benedicts a piece of her mind. She didn't need or want an armed, frowning behemoth following her around everywhere she went. Bad enough there was one here, watching her every move as she got out of her car and headed to the elevator.

The door of the penthouse across the hall opened just as she exited the elevator.

"Hey, pretty Penelope, want to come over and play?" Josh stood with his arms folded over his chest, one eyebrow raised, and a smile that was too cute by half.

"After you saddled me with a babysitter this afternoon?" She gave him a good frown to let him know she hadn't appreciated his actions.

Josh's smile vanished. He stepped forward, put his hands on her waist, and lifted her right up so that her face was level with his.

"I'm not going to apologize for doing everything I can to keep you safe. You matter. So deal with it."

Penelope forgot about protesting when his mouth claimed hers. His flavor intoxicated her, completely eroding every thought from her mind. Helpless to resist him, she wrapped her arms around his neck and kissed him back. Their tongues swirled and danced. How could she be so instantly and totally aroused?

He carried her, but it wasn't until he weaned his lips from hers and began kissing her neck that she realized he'd brought her into his apartment.

"Oh." Apparently Josh's kisses managed to short-circuit her brain, if that was the only thing she could say.

"I missed you today." Josh set her down then tilted her face up to his. "I really missed you."

"I missed you, too." That was the truth, and compartmentalization be damned. Before she could say another word, Alex laid his hands on her shoulders and then turned her into his arms.

His expression looked so hopeful, she said, "And I missed you, too." She didn't wait, just went up on her toes so she could taste him, so she could drown in his flavor and revel in the heat of his embrace.

Josh moved in behind her, his heat as potent as his brother's. He stroked her, random caresses that gave pleasure and created a hunger for more.

Penelope ended her kiss with Alex, then tilted her head so she could mate her mouth with Josh's again. When she came up for air, he took her hand.

"Come to bed with us, sweetheart," Josh said.

Why couldn't she resist them?

Because I don't want to.

No, she didn't want to resist any opportunity to be with these men, to touch and taste, to tease and ease and celebrate. Whenever they loved, whenever they stripped down and simply immersed themselves in pleasure, such joy filled her, she knew it had to overflow to fill them, too.

They reached the bedroom, and Penelope began to undress, letting her clothing drop where it would. She needed no seduction. She wanted this, would take this for herself. They made her greedy for all the pleasure she could grab. Passion like this couldn't last, could it? No, of course not. So she would take it all while she could and deal with the consequences later.

She would deal with the fact she'd fallen in love with these two honchos in the after time. After the fire faded. After they'd moved on.

"You make me so hard."

Josh reached out and helped her step out of her slacks. Then he cupped her, the heat of his hand flooding her cunt with desire. He slipped his fingers behind the crotch of her panties and penetrated her.

"And you get so wet for us." He bent down and kissed her, his tongue tangling with hers in a way that left no doubt as to his intentions. His fingers worked in the same rhythm as his tongue.

Alex ran his hand down her back, played it across her ass, then began to run his fingers up and down the crack of her ass.

"Will you let us take you here?" Alex's request made her heart race. Imagining having them deep inside her that way had been firing her blood since they'd inserted the butt plug in her. She craved to have them every way she could have them, one at a time and together.

"Yes. Yes. I want it all."

"Jesus, you're a wonder." Alex kissed her shoulder.

Josh captured her mouth with his. She kissed him, sinking into him, and she reached for Alex, feeling his flesh under her hand, the heat of him.

Josh's lips left hers and trailed down the column of her throat. Tilting her head back, she opened herself to him, silently urging him to take all that she had to give him. She inhaled deeply and could smell them, the aroma of the two of them intertwined, combined, into the most sensual of fragrances.

Their scent and their taste had become necessary to her, a tonic that steadied her and thrilled her, that made her whole.

Alex kissed her as Josh tongued her nipple. Her hands gladly stroked and petted, the sensation of hot flesh over hard, honed muscle one that fed her inner female. Here, under her hands, lay the proof that those bigger and stronger than her had a power over her. This sensation harkened back to the past, to a time when the hunters, the protectors of the human species demanded and received fealty as their due.

Hardly a righteous thought for a modern woman. No, but a part of her, that part which was purely physical and instinctual, recognized the truth in it.

Her tongue played with Alex's, and her hand fisted him, held the essence of his masculinity in her palm and felt elated he gave it to her, for her pleasure.

Alex's mouth left hers. He wrapped his arms around her from behind, as if bracing her.

Josh stroked his hand over the opening of her slit and then speared two fingers into her. Groaning in bliss, Penelope rode those fingers as they moved in and out of her. Her nipples hardened, a visceral reaction to the arousal shimmering through her.

"Oh, yeah, you're hot, wet, and ready." Josh placed a kiss on her navel then sank to his knees. "I'm going to drink some of your heat, pretty Penelope."

His last words vibrated against her pussy, and then he set his mouth on her, lips and tongue rubbing, tasting, devouring her. Arousal burst into flames high and hot, searing her flesh and electrifying every part of her. She cried out because the burn happened so fast, shooting her higher and farther in seconds, carrying her close, so close to rapture. Alex held her steady, taking her weight when her knees buckled. She could feel his cock nestled against the small of her back, and she loved the feeling—hot, pulsing, preparing itself for her.

Josh's tongue flicked over her labia, teasing her clit from its nest. Penelope shivered as her excitement grew.

"You taste so good."

Oh, his words spoken against her wet cleft felt so delicious, she tilted her hips just a little bit closer to him.

"Please." She hungered, she burned. She knew she'd become sopping wet and knew, too, those juices weren't all from his wonderful mouth.

"Here, then." He inserted fingers into her again, then sucked her clit into his mouth.

"Oh, *yes!*" She came in a torrent, a flood of ecstasy so grand, so thrilling, she wondered her heart didn't stop. Controlling her completely, the orgasm wrung sobs and sounds from the very heart of her, turning her inside out, leaving her a heaving, quivering woman.

Joshua got to his feet, scooped her up, and laid her on the bed. He came down over top of her and laid his mouth on hers, sharing her essence, the flavor of them both, in his kiss. He reached for a condom, never taking his gaze from hers as he tore the package open, rolled on the rubber, and surged into her.

Penelope gasped, the length and the girth of him stretching her, the strength of his cock as he withdrew then thrust into her again so awesomely powerful, so powerfully good.

"You feel good inside me." She wrapped her arms and legs around him and pushed up against his thrusts. Penelope thought their movements were just this side of desperate.

"Oh, sweetheart, yes, I just need—" He closed his eyes, a sign he was close to release. She stretched up, fastened her mouth on his neck, and sucked—an old-fashioned ploy she'd never tried on any man. These men brought out the primitive in her, the need to mark them as her own.

Josh made a sound, half groan, half growl, and Penelope used her inner muscles to squeeze him, to push him over the edge. She held him close as he came, as his orgasm robbed him of strength, and wondered that such a moment made a woman feel so powerful and special.

He collapsed on her, breathing hard, but only for a moment. These lovers of hers were both so careful of her, for in just a few short breaths, he raised himself onto his arms, sparing her his weight.

"I'm wrecked."

Penelope chuckled, the idea that a strong man would say such a thing tickling her sense of humor.

"Maybe for a moment you are, but I have seen your powers of regeneration, sir, and they are remarkable."

"No, you're remarkable." He eased out of her, off of her, and rolled to her right.

Alex cozied up to her left side. He rubbed his hand over her breasts, first one, then the other. "Your nipples are rock hard. I think you're still up there. I think you need more, pretty Penelope."

Penelope turned her head toward him. "I'm horny," she said baldly. "What are you going to do about it?"

Alex nuzzled her, his tongue sneaking out to tease her ear. She shivered as she always did when he did that.

"I'm going to have my way with you and show you so many fireworks you'll think it's the Fourth of July."

"That's quite an impressive boast."

"I can be quite the impressive lover."

Penelope wanted to laugh. She loved this playful side of Alex, loved that he would put on the mantle of a Lothario to make her smile. She'd always thought that here, in bed, there should be more than just the heated pursuit of orgasms. There should be tenderness and, yes, humor.

"Go ahead. Impress me."

Alex grinned in response to her sultry tone. He reached out, stroked her face, then leaned in to kiss her.

Gentle at first, his lips wooed hers, his tongue stroked gently, begging her to open to him. Unable to resist, she surrendered, his taste, now wrapped in the scent of cooling bodies and spent sex, even more alluring, even more potent.

He moved over her, his mouth avid in tasting, teasing, taking what he would. Penelope closed her eyes in bliss as he left not an inch of her unloved. His hands caressed and shaped, fingers delved, and she lifted her hips, following that touch, crying out for that taste.

When he eased her over on her stomach, she went, moaning with delight as he kissed a trail from the top of her spine down to the tiny dimple at the top of her ass. He moved, his heat emanating off him in waves, so she felt comforted and aroused at the same time. He tented her, his hands on either side of her head, his knees on either side of her legs. He urged her bottom up, and she raised herself for him, for his pleasure, and for her own. One leg pressed, and she spread hers, opening her body to him, becoming, for him, completely vulnerable.

Heat on her right side made her turn her head. Josh lay there, close, propped up on his side. His eyes glittered with excitement. She opened her mouth to comment on his recovery, then closed it on a hiss.

Alex's fingers traced up and down over her anus, spreading a cool lubricant, shooting her arousal even higher.

"I'll be careful, sweetheart." Alex bent down and kissed her shoulder, and then he inserted a finger into her ass.

"Oh." She couldn't believe how sensitive she was there, how, instantly, threads of almost electric energy shot from her anus to her clit and up to her nipples.

Josh leaned over, placed a chaste kiss on her cheek. He reached out, and in a breath of time, she felt his fingers on her slit, rubbing back and forth, seeking and finding her clit.

"Mmm." The twin stimulations worked together, not pushing her over, but seeming to expand what she could take, how high she could soar. "I love this."

"Staying high, like a kite?" Alex asked.

"Yes. Yes! I love coming, but this…mmm." Words fell away, giving over to the sensory stimulation that swirled and pleasured and teased.

"A bit more, baby." Alex's voice seemed to quiver. She felt additional pressure and guessed he'd given her a second finger. The burning hovered at the edge of pain, but even the discomfort aroused. Nothing had ever felt like this.

"You want this, don't you? It's like your ass is just opening for me."

"Yes, I want this. I want you. Please, fuck me. Fuck my ass."

"Oh, yeah." His voice did quiver. She heard the sound of the condom pack being opened and the distinctive glide as he rolled the protection into place.

"You can tell me to stop, sweetheart. Anytime. I don't want to hurt you."

It was on the tip of her tongue to assure him she would never ask him to stop. And then she felt it, the hot, huge end of his cock pressing against her. His hands gripped her ass, spread her cheeks just a little, and the pressure grew.

She inhaled sharply, as the slight burn she'd felt morphed into a stretching burn that nearly brought tears to her eyes. But the sound she made wasn't one of distress. She recognized the noise even though she'd never made one like it. It was a plea for more.

"Let go, sweetheart. Let go for me." Alex bent down and kissed her shoulder.

She felt her sphincter open, a little at a time. The burn turned to pain, and she nearly clenched against it. And then she realized she was clenched, and that's what Alex had asked her to let go of.

She pressed herself against Josh's hand, sought more of the stimulation that kept her high, kept her needy, even as she willed her muscles to relax, to give over—to let go.

"Oh, baby, yes." Alex's words slid out of him as his cock slid into her. He inhaled sharply and held himself still.

"Penelope?"

"Move."

"Out?"

"God, no. Move!" She thought she'd explode if he didn't fuck her, if he didn't…

"I'll go slowly." He pulled nearly all the way out then pushed back in again, a small movement that felt good, oh, but not nearly good enough. She needed more. She needed so much more. Instinctively, she pushed back, just a little, meeting his thrust, meeting it and taking him deeper.

"I can't control…sweetheart, hold still…" His voice strangled off on a curse.

Penelope didn't want to hold still. She thrust back again, taking more of him until she had taken him all.

"Oh, God."

She could almost hear the tether of his control snap. He held her ass harder and thrust into her, then out and in again, this time his pace sharp, fast.

Penelope felt the spasms of climax hover. Then Josh moved closer and inserted two fingers into her pussy.

"Come for us, sweetheart."

"Yes." Her one word ended in a hiss and a cry as her release flooded her, an inundation of sensation so huge, so massive, it stole her breath and her sight and her hearing. She came in wave after wave of the most delectable ecstasy, shivering and sobbing as the orgasm drowned all that she was, a purging pleasure that changed every atom of her being. She felt Alex hold himself deep, the vibration of his sobs of triumph shivering over her, and knew she wasn't the only one changed.

As he eased himself down on top of her, as she absorbed the heat from his body and Josh's gentle, comforting sounds, she understood something irreversible had just happened.

The brothers Benedict had just claimed a portion of her soul, and she'd fallen all the way in love with them.

Chapter 14

Alex's legs burned, his lungs struggled for air, and sweat ran down his back between his shoulder blades. He preferred exercise the old-fashioned way—either riding his horse across miles of Texas pasture, or slugging away on the ranch. The exercise room in Benedict Towers came in a distant third in preferences, but the workout had value despite that.

Beside him, Josh was having a very similar reaction to his elliptical program. Alex put his attention back on the television screen above him, only half-listening to the news program. He and Josh weren't competing, but they matched each other's pace and effort in most things.

Some of the people he'd met in college had been siblings—hell, some even twins. They all suffered to some degree from sibling rivalry. He guessed the difference was how they'd been raised.

He'd clicked with Josh as soon as he'd been old enough to understand that he could like one brother a whole lot more than either of the other two. The feeling had been mutual. He considered his brother Josh—one year his senior—to be his partner, not his rival.

In many ways, they were like two versions of the same person.

Alex checked the time and saw he only had a couple of minutes left to go. Thoughts of Penelope intruded, and he lost his rhythm. She'd been prettily mussed and sleepy-warm when their sister Susan had called earlier, inviting her to go shopping.

"You okay?" Josh had stopped his workout and leaned on the instrument panel.

"Yeah."

"Penelope?"

"Yeah." Alex smiled. It was pretty good when your best friend was your brother who understood you completely.

"Want to hit the pool?"

"No, let's head up. I need coffee."

They scooped their towels and water bottles and headed for the penthouse elevator. Not many of their fellow apartment dwellers were out and about this Saturday morning. They sometimes would encounter people in the corridors or in the workout room, or the pool, but never in the elevators. Unless, of course, one of the family was visiting.

"So tell me, bro, what's on your mind about Penelope?" Josh headed straight to their one-cup coffee machine. He scooped two coffee pods—one would be a breakfast blend for Alex, one a medium blend for himself.

They did have a few differences in tastes and preferences.

"I've been feeling as if we're, I don't know, taking Penelope for granted."

"Because every time we're alone with her, we're on her and in her? I've been having the same thoughts."

"We brought food over to her place the other night, but other than that we haven't taken her anywhere. Not to dinner and a movie. Not to the symphony. That's not our usual style. We can do better than that. Hell, she's brand new to the state *and* to the city, and we haven't shown her any of it."

"I don't know what it is about her that's so different from any other woman we've ever dated." Josh handed Alex his coffee then set about making his own.

"I know. It's like we met her, then, bang, we leapfrog over all the steps in between meeting and sex and jump her the first night."

"Do you have any idea what we could do to maybe balance it out a bit? Aside from not having sex with her because at this point, I don't know if I can leave her alone."

"I feel the same way." Alex took a sip from his coffee, and then smiled. "I know. Since we haven't heard from Lola about dinner tonight at Sorrento's, let's take Penelope there. We do have the reservation, and it is for three."

"Good thinking. And if Lola *does* call us back, we'll just tell her that since we didn't hear from her, we made other arrangements."

"That feels better. Penelope deserves to go out and about."

"Do you want me to see if I can get us some tickets for the symphony?" Josh asked. Alex knew that procuring tickets even the day of wasn't a problem for a Benedict. They could always use the family box, but that usually was arranged with the Town Trust well ahead of time, since any member of the families was entitled to do so.

"Yeah. I have no idea what they're performing, but they're bound to be playing something classy tonight." Alex smiled, because it felt good to be planning a night out with Penelope. Then he frowned. "Maybe I should call her and make sure she's okay with these plans."

"Really good thinking! Women sometimes don't take to these kinds of last-minute surprises the way we men believe they should." Josh sighed. "It's just one of the things I don't get about them."

Alex pulled out his cell phone while Josh pulled out his. They walked away from each other in order to make the separate calls. Alex felt much better now that he and Josh were going to take Penelope out. Sorrento's and the symphony. An evening with taste and style. What could be better?

* * * *

"You look shell-shocked. Bad news?" Susan Benedict came back from searching one of the racks of casual dresses. She had a couple more hangers holding dresses in her hands that she'd obviously selected, not for herself, but for Penelope.

Penelope had never met a woman who liked to shop the way Susan did.

She slid her cell phone back into her jeans pocket. "Your brother, Alex, just called. He and Josh have invited me out with the two of them tonight. Someplace called Sorrento's, and then on to the symphony."

"*Tonight.*" Susan proved her intelligence by honing in on the one word that had Penelope feeling in a panic.

"Yes. Tonight. They'll pick me up at six."

"I hope you told them no, and that next time they could give you more advance notice. Damn it, those two really don't have a clue when it comes to women."

Penelope felt her face heating. "I was going to say no. I *meant* to say no." She sighed. She didn't want to agree with Susan's assessment of her brothers, because they certainly had more than a clue as to how to heat her up and turn her on.

But Susan had a point. For all that they could make her melt in mere seconds flat, Josh and Alex seemed to be somewhat socially inept.

Penelope sighed again. That was a condition she could relate to, as she'd never been particularly adroit in that area herself. When she looked up to see Susan looking at her, she thought that maybe a partial confession was in order. "I can't seem to say no to those two. At any time at all, for anything. Ever."

"Oh." Susan's mouth formed a perfect O. When Penelope just looked at her, she snapped it shut.

"You and my brothers?" She sounded incredulous. Then she smiled. "Well, that's…good. Really! I like you. And, you're okay with…" She let her words drop off, her hand waving to indicate, well, it could be anything and everything, but Penelope understood what she meant.

"I grew up hearing stories of your family every time Grandma Kate came to visit. So the idea of a ménage relationship isn't as foreign to me as it might be to someone else. And although I'd never before taken two lovers at the same time, I'm fine with it." Now her face did heat. "Um, more than fine, and maybe we can get back to the matter of my upcoming date tonight, because it's a little embarrassing to be talking about this here, in Neiman Marcus, and with you, their sister."

"Okay. But maybe we'll grab lunch one day next week, in your office, and you can tell all." Susan wore such a wickedly overdone leer on her face Penelope laughed.

"I'm not sure I want to dish to you about sex with your brothers. But we'll definitely have lunch."

Susan grinned. "Kelsey felt the same way, but I eventually wormed some details out of her."

"I'm made of sterner stuff. Half old England, half New England." Then she shook her head. "I can only imagine what sort of restaurant Sorrento's is. Very good, very posh."

"And very welcoming," Susan said. "It's one of Grandma Kate's favorite places to eat in Houston. Not at all stuffy."

"Then there's the symphony. That black dress I bought today should do for tonight. I was going to wait to buy some bling to go with it. But I think I'm going to have to do that, now."

"Let's get you a couple more outfits first. Then we'll go after accessories and bling."

Penelope could afford to splurge on herself, but she found a lifetime of living frugally difficult to overcome. Her grandmother had left her very well-off. That had surprised her at the time because while they'd lived well, they hadn't lived lavishly.

Penelope missed her grandmother. The older woman had never heaped a lot of affection on her, but Penelope had come to know, over time, that she could count on Eloise Wright to be there for her, day in and day out, no matter what.

That steadiness, that solidity, had healed her after the cruel rejection of her mother. After her grandmother's funeral, she'd discovered that her Gram had sent periodic letters to Chloe Primrose Smitherman, but had received very few in return.

As far as Penelope was concerned, the woman who had given birth to her could stay on the other side of the Atlantic Ocean forever. She wanted no part of her.

"Wow, you look pissed. Should I warn my brothers?"

Penelope shook her head. "Sorry. My thoughts wandered to unhappy territory."

She wouldn't splurge overmuch, but she *would* see to it that when the brothers Benedict called for her this evening, they'd swallow their tongues.

* * * *

A few hours later when she opened her door in response to the doorbell, Penelope decided the money she'd just spent had been well worth it.

She had been going to wear the all-occasion little black dress she'd purchased at Macy's, until she'd found the silk kimono dress in rich cornflower blue. On the hanger, the garment had looked deceptively demure. On her, it was a whole other story. The silk clung in all the right places, and the slit over her left thigh teased unmercifully. The silver accents on the dress itself had limited the need for bling. She'd swept her hair up using subtle pins and a pair of chopsticks to complement the exotic look.

Both men's mouths dropped open when they saw her, and that, Penelope thought, was certainly worth every dollar she'd spent.

"Wow. You tempt us to keep you here, all to ourselves," Josh said.

"We're going to have to protect you from all the men who are certain to vie for your attention." Alex's words had come out softer, as if he hadn't meant to say them aloud.

"You can't offer me a night out with Italian food and music, and then renege." She gave them a smile that felt sultry. "And as far as I'm concerned, there won't be any other men. Shall we go?"

Penelope felt charmed from the moment they stepped out of the lobby of Benedict Towers. The men had arranged for a limousine. The car came equipped with a bar, and Josh made a great ceremony of pouring them each a glass of champagne.

"I'm completely uneducated when it comes to wine and fine dining," she confessed. She took a sip of the bubbly.

"Ah, well, this is a Louis Roederer Cristal Brut, 2002, of which one wine review characterized as insolent, brash, and earthbound. That's a direct quote," Josh said.

"Which magazine?" Alex asked.

"*Wine & Spirits.*"

Penelope hid her smile behind her glass. She really wasn't much of a wine drinker, period, but liked the hint of citrus in this champagne.

Before she'd had more than a few more sips, they arrived at the restaurant. The sense of otherworldly enchantment continued as she took in the building, and as they went inside. She felt transported to a villa in Italy, with piano music, soft voices, and gentle lighting.

"Ah, Signors Benedict, *benvenuto a* Sorrento Ristorante Italiano!"

"Hello, Maria, how are you tonight?" Alex smiled and nodded, and kept one arm protectively around Penelope's waist.

"Very well, sir. Your table is ready, of course."

The young woman led them to a table set for three, in a dining room that featured a painting that took up an entire wall, of incredible blue water and a slice of coast, likely a depiction of the city for which the restaurant was named.

"Enjoy your meal." Maria bowed slightly as she left.

Josh noticed her looking at the painting. "Have you ever been to Italy?" he asked.

"No. The extent of my worldly travels were when I flew from London to America, and most recently, came from New York to here."

"We realize that we haven't taken the time to get to know you." Alex looked around as if to ensure no one was paying them any attention. "At least, not outside of the bedroom. Grandma Kate said you were raised by your maternal grandmother? That must have been hard, losing your parents when you were so young."

Penelope rarely spoke of her past, simply because to do so not only always felt uncomfortable, but often left her feeling raw and angry.

She'd used several lines to gloss over her history, and most people didn't pry any further. Since it felt very much as if the brothers Benedict wanted to move this relationship to another level, she decided to be honest with them.

"I didn't lose my parents in the way I think you mean. I never knew my father, as he died of a drug overdose before I was born. And as for my mother, when I turned ten, she met a man, a wealthy man who had no interest in having anything to do with another man's child. So she sent me to live with her mother, my grandmother, whom I'd never met."

"Your own mother sent you away so she could be with a *man*?"

Josh's obvious outrage soothed Penelope in ways she couldn't define. She nodded. "Chloe Primrose Smitherman is very good at looking out for herself. I understand she and *his nibs* have a beautiful home in Wiltshire, and a couple of children, to boot."

"I can't tolerate a man who won't man up," Alex said. His tone matched his brother's. He picked up her hand and kissed it. "I'm sorry you went through that," he said.

"But if you hadn't, we might never have met you," Josh said.

Penelope felt her throat tighten. Before she could respond, she sensed movement behind her. She saw only a flash of red, and the sudden white, worried expressions on the men's faces.

Penelope thought the blonde looked demure, despite her rather impressive bosom. That impression melted away as she picked up a glass of wine from the next table and tossed it in Alex's face.

"So, this is the tramp you threw me over for?" the woman all but screamed. "Does she know she's a candidate for your Legacy Project? That you want to make her your brood mare?"

Chapter 15

Oh, shit.

Joshua surged to his feet, outrage warring with embarrassment as he faced the very pissed-off, very buxom blonde. His brain scrambled, trying to analyze the best tact to take to prevent an all-out disaster. In a sudden explosion of insight, he realized it wouldn't do for Penelope to find out about the Legacy Project. No, that wouldn't do at all.

"Ms. Dell. I'll have to ask you to leave." Of course, he didn't have to ask that, as two of the heftier waiters were rushing toward them to do that very thing. As well, several men were on their feet. Of course, Josh didn't know if they were getting ready to pitch in and help him or were just trying to get a better look at Lola's décolletage.

"You can ask all you want. I'm going to let it be known far and wide what kind of nefarious plan the two of you sickos have been hatching. I've heard stories about that place you come from out there in the middle of nowhere. I've heard about the orgies that happen all over the damn place and how women are treated like things, little better than animals. Well, I'm having none of it!"

Joshua took note of two things at once. The first was that Lola looked perilously close to tears. The second was that Penelope, whose shocked expression had turned curious, was fast edging toward outrage herself.

It was likely the slur against the town that did that, he thought.

If Joshua didn't do something soon, an all-out catfight might happen, and while there was an adolescent part of him that got excited at that prospect, his adult self fully understood such a thing might be his and Alex's own personal flaming Waterloo.

When in doubt, go on the indignant attack.

"I don't know what you're talking about, Ms. Dell, or where you get your information. I suggest you leave now, before this situation escalates into one with litigious ramifications."

The woman shouldn't have looked as if she didn't understand him, considering she'd graduated Phi Beta Kappa and held two separate master's degrees in business administration and accounting. One thing was certain. This incident had taken her off the Legacy list completely.

No way in hell either he or Alex wanted a wife given to public displays.

"Madam, we must ask you to leave immediately. Otherwise, we will have no choice but to call the police."

Joshua thought it was the mention of the cops that got Lola's attention. Still furious, she gave them the finger, said, "fuck you, assholes," and, with an escort on either side of her, left their table and the restaurant.

Another server had rushed over with a towel to help Alex mop up the Riesling he was wearing.

"Thank God that gentleman wasn't drinking a nice red Merlot," Alex said.

Once they were alone again, Penelope turned her attention to Joshua. "Who was that woman?"

"Ms. Lola Dell is an accountant with the firm of Johnson, Dyson, and Howe, here in Houston." Joshua recalled times when he'd been called on the carpet for one imagined crime or another. He and all his siblings had always had a pact. Volunteer nothing, offer only what is asked for. He reverted to that strategy now.

"But why was she angry?" Penelope seemed totally bewildered. "What was she talking about? What Legacy Project? I mean, that's a bit extreme, isn't it? Tracking someone down at a tony restaurant and causing such a public scene? She must have thought she had a very good reason."

Joshua felt as if he was sinking, fast. Maybe that "volunteer nothing" policy wasn't such a good idea, after all. He turned to Alex, hoping his more inventive brother would jump in and help.

"We've been planning branching off into some diverse fields," Alex said. "You know, renewable sources of energy, trying to find the very best venue to take the company into the future."

All that was true. They *had* been talking about the merits of solar and wind power, and structuring a brand-new division of Benedict Oil and Minerals.

"And you were calling that the Legacy Project! Because you were protecting the legacy of future generations by developing green energies!"

"Um…yes. Exactly. And we were looking at hiring some new talent, um, from outside the oil industry, as…" Alex looked like he'd come to the end of his inventive streak.

Joshua cleared his throat. "As they'd be more likely to look at everything from a different perspective, as it were. Thinking outside the oil company, um…box."

"I wonder where she got the idea that you were looking for a brood mare? That's totally strange, isn't it?"

"The woman called you a tramp and said we have orgies and subjugate our women," Alex reminded her. "It's all strange, if you ask me."

"I'd suggest you don't hire Ms. Dell," Penelope said. "I don't think the woman is stable."

"Don't worry," Alex said. "That little display definitely took her out of the running."

"Amen," Joshua said. It was time to try and put this incident behind them. "Have you decided what you'll have? How about an appetizer? I love their wild mushroom risotto. It's served with white truffle oil and from a carved Grana Padana wheel."

"Yes, it says that right here on the menu. What is a Grana Padana wheel?" Penelope asked.

"Parmesan cheese," Alex said.

"Oh. That sounds good. And I want the lobster bisque."

"Theirs is one of the best," Joshua said.

The waiter came, apologized for the disturbance, then took their orders. Joshua began to relax. He had the sense that he and his brother had just dodged a major train wreck. He also had the feeling they weren't out of the woods yet. One look at Alex and he knew they'd have to discuss this entire situation—not just Ms. Dell, but the Legacy Project, itself.

Sooner, rather than later.

* * * *

Penelope felt extremely relaxed by the time the limousine pulled up to Benedict Towers. They'd come back here after dinner so Alex could hurry upstairs and change his shirt. Then they'd made the symphony on time.

She hadn't wanted to admit that she really didn't know much about classical music, either. But she'd enjoyed the performance, nonetheless. They'd had some more champagne at intermission, and both men had been sweetly attentive.

She wasn't drunk, not by a long shot. But she was very mellow.

The men didn't say anything as they headed inside. She found herself holding hands with them both, and liked it.

"Thank you both. I had a wonderful time tonight."

"You're welcome," Josh said.

Once inside the elevator, Alex reached over and tilted her chin up with one finger. He kissed her, the touch of his mouth on hers light, his tongue just gently brushing her lips as if he simply wanted to taste her.

"Will you come home with us? Will you be with us?"

There was nothing Penelope wanted more. She wanted to lie naked with these men, to touch them, taste them, and be touched and tasted in turn. She wanted to give them pleasure and wallow in the delight they would give to her. She wanted to feel them both inside her.

Penelope licked her lips, letting Alex know she tasted him, too. Her stomach fluttered because she wanted more than *just* to be with them. "Yes. Yes, please. And I want—" Her words caught in her throat because what she wanted was the very embodiment of the dream that had haunted her, the dream that had aroused her and made every man she'd met, before these two, seem lacking.

"What is it you want, angel? You have to know we'll give you anything you want, if we can." Josh's words brushed her forehead, his kiss there warming her and calming her nerves.

"I want to have you both inside me at the same time."

"Are you sure?" Alex's hands trembled as he cupped her face, as he lifted her so his gaze could meet hers. In his eyes she read excitement and hope.

"I'm sure. I want everything. I want it all."

"Sweetheart." Josh gathered her in and kissed her, his mouth warm and wet, the slide of his lips and the probe of his tongue lighting fires that had been banked all evening, just from spending time with them.

The elevator doors opened, and together they moved down the corridor and entered the men's penthouse.

She didn't need seduction, but oh, how lovely it was that they took the time to give it to her. Alex kissed her, drawing her in, drawing her close, his arms sure and snug around her, his lips wooing hers.

Penelope let herself sink into his kiss, into the slide of lips and thrust of tongue, into the heat and the magic. Alex eased back and just looked at her, his eyes shining, making her melt. He caressed her cheek. She tilted her head, leaned into his touch, and felt very kittenish.

The scent of lavender and lemon surrounded her from the candles Josh lit. Music, soft and dreamy jazz, filled the air.

Josh came to her then, turned her into his arms, and mated his mouth to hers. He tasted slightly of the brandy he'd sipped earlier, and raw, potent male. She would know his kiss blindfolded, would be able to distinguish him from his brother by touch, taste, and aroma any place, any time.

The heat of Alex's body blanketed her back, so that between them they cocooned her in a world of sensual promise. The scent of them enveloped her, arousing her, so that her slit slickened and her nipples hardened.

"You're so responsive to us, Penelope. Do you have any idea what a turn-on that is for us?" Joshua used one finger to trace the pucker of her nipple against the silk of her dress.

"I can't help it. Right from the first moment I set eyes on the two of you, you've done this to me." She wanted to tell them so much more than that. She'd fallen in love with them both. They'd charmed her and intrigued her. Their shy intelligence so matched her own sense of herself. Though born to wealth and privilege, they were beguilingly humble. She longed to tell them how she felt, yet the fear of rejection—that horrible legacy from her childhood—held her back and kept her silent.

"For us, too." Alex caressed her arms and slid his hands down to entwine his fingers with hers.

"This is special." Josh cupped her face and placed a gentle, chaste kiss on her lips. "You're special." He eased her toward him, and she willingly went, stretching up on her toes to taste his mouth again.

Behind her, Alex eased the zipper of her dress down. She shrugged her shoulders, letting the garment slide from her body.

"You're trying to kill us," Josh whispered.

Penelope smiled. The ultra-sexy red lace teddy she'd bought just that afternoon had felt like sin when she'd put it on earlier. Seeing the way Josh's eyes widened, the way his nostrils flared as his gaze devoured her, told her she'd more than made the right choice.

"Lord, woman, you're hot." Alex's praise whispered against her ear. He used his tongue to tease the shell of it, something that always made her shiver with delicious anticipation.

"You make me hot, the two of you. Only the two you. No one else has ever made me melt." It was as close as she dared come to saying the words out loud, to declaring her love.

Josh's gaze heated her. "This is very sexy, but, darling, it has got to go." He skimmed the teddy down, his hands making quick work of stripping her. He moved his right hand between her thighs, stroking over her slit, and then slid two fingers inside her.

"Oh, yes, so hot and wet and *ready* for us." He leaned forward and took her mouth with his. There was nothing chaste about this kiss. Hot, hungry, his lips sucked hers, his tongue invaded, an in-and-out drinking that took her arousal so high she barely recognized the sounds she made. She tilted her hips into his thrusting fingers, seeking more, needing more. Her hands grabbed his shoulders, and if she could have climbed him then, she knew she would have.

Hands from behind slid around her waist, gently easing her back against hot, naked male flesh.

Josh's fingers left her and she whimpered.

"Let him get undressed, angel," Alex whispered. "We're going to take very good care of you, I promise."

"I need you both so much. I need you to hold me and eat me and fuck me." Never had Penelope spoken so brazenly. The emotions, the needs swirling through her, felt raw and primitive. They pulled and pushed inside her until she thought she might scream if she didn't get what she needed.

"All that and more." Josh stepped forward, gloriously naked, his clothes abandoned in a messy, discarded heap. "You'll have all that and more, sweetheart. Starting right now."

He lifted her into his arms, and she wrapped herself around him, relishing the sensation of flesh against flesh. His cock, so hard and hot and big, nestled between the lips of her pussy as if it knew that's exactly where it belonged.

He laid her on the bed and came down beside her on her right. Alex stretched out on her left. How wonderful it felt to have these hot, naked men surrounding her. Her pussy gushed, ecstatic with their nearness. Her nipples beaded, turning so hard they almost hurt.

"We need you, too," Josh said as he stroked his hand down her body. He petted her with one long caress from neck to thighs. "We've had women before. We've shared women before. But nothing has ever been like it has been with you. With you, it's so much more than just sex. It's deeper, sweeter, hotter. We don't understand it, either, but it is, and we're glad."

"When we're lying here like this, there's something that feels as if we've always been together." Alex's voice, low and deep, seemed to vibrate deep in her stomach. "It's a kind of recognition of what we are, the three of us, collectively. That sense of unity is something we've never experienced before."

"Please." Their words were undoing her, making her feel shaky, urging her to step out onto that emotional limb. Drawing her away from the here and now, because a part of her believed if she took that chance, if she stepped out onto that limb, she would never, ever recover the rejection that was certain to follow.

So much better to bury everything under a thick layer of sex and sensations.

Their hands brushed so close to her clit. Penelope undulated her hips, trying to entice them to stroke her there even as she reached down and wrapped a hand around each of their cocks.

Hot, hard, and silky, the feel of them thrilled, the girth of them whet her appetite and drove her even higher.

"You'd have us off like rockets," Alex said. "But it's our turn to drive you crazy."

He reached down and freed himself from her grasp. Then, before she could draw another breath, he slid down the bed and buried his face between her legs.

Penelope groaned, her eyes closing on the first delicious sweep of his tongue against her cunt. She lifted herself, pushing into his mouth, and he responded by using lips and teeth and tongue to excite her, to drink from her and send her on a thrilling climb toward bliss.

Josh turned her face to him and kissed her, sucking on her mouth in a rhythm that matched his brother's.

Higher, faster, she imagined herself a speeding bolt of energy, gaining strength, racing toward the sun. Penelope pulled her mouth away from Josh, crying out as her orgasm shimmered just on the horizon. Alex slowed his actions, adjusting himself on the bed, and she had one moment to realize he'd put on a condom. Then he surged up her body and plunged into her in a single deep thrust.

Penelope came in a starburst of sensation, wave after wave of rapture consuming her, making her heart pound and her thoughts scatter.

Alex reversed their positions, then pulled her mouth down to kiss her, to share the taste of her pussy with her. The flavor of them combined enthralled her, making her crave more.

Josh moved in behind her, and when he urged, she gained her knees. Straddling Alex with his cock still buried deep inside her, she eased her lips from him, took one moment to look over her shoulder.

"Do you want me to fuck your ass?" Josh's voice had gone husky.

"Yes. Oh, yes. Right now."

She shivered when he ran his lube-coated fingers up and down the crack of her ass, and shivered when he moved closer, placed his hands on her cheeks, and spread her slightly.

Then he pressed against her anus.

Alex drew her head down, slipped his arms around her. Holding her for his brother's penetration.

Burning, stretching, Penelope inhaled deeply as the pressure built, as the burn turned to a fine, biting pain. The sensation rekindled her arousal, a fast, sharp rise that made her mew in pleasure and need.

"Do you want me to stop?"

"No! Give me more."

"Then let go, sweetheart. Let go and let me take you," Josh said.

Alex stroked his hand down her back, and Penelope relaxed, giving Josh the surrender he demanded.

She felt herself stretching, a steady growing pain that made her pussy clench and her nipples harden. And then she felt him slide in, all the way in.

"Oh, God, hold still." Josh's whisper sounded tortured.

Penelope couldn't hold still. The sensations of Eros, the thrill and the tingle and the snapping sizzle went beyond her control, growing, spreading, taking her over the top into explosive, all-consuming climax.

She screamed as she came, her body clenching and releasing, every muscle contracting at once.

"God!" Both men cursed, both began to move inside her as the rapture that seized her pulled them in.

On and on the shivering ecstasy burned, as she gasped and cried and let it carry her away completely.

Chapter 16

It feels like Black Monday.

Alex tried to put his finger on the source of nervous dread that ran through him. He could find no logical reason to feel this way. The weekend had been beyond his wildest dreams of perfect. He'd awakened this very morning with Penelope snuggled close to him. The three of them had enjoyed a hot, steamy shower followed by hot, steamy sex. He should be feeling on top of the world.

His glance flicked to his desk calendar, and he had the sense he should remember the date. Black Monday, indeed.

Alex didn't know why his subconscious was so quick to assign such a negative moniker to the day. He decided to take a few minutes and look at the situation analytically. True, there'd been a few fires to put out since he'd arrived at the office that morning, but nothing he wasn't able to handle in his usual competent style. The feud in the marketing department—thanks to a love affair turned sour—had been the toughest, but even that situation had eventually been diffused. The sudden, no-notice-given departure of one of the junior accountants just before month end he personally put down to that debacle at Sorrento's on Saturday night, as no other explanation made any sense at all.

The company had an extremely low turnover rate.

It seemed a logical assumption that Ms. Dell, the president of one of the local professional accountants' associations would be acquainted with Ms. Selma Bracket, late of the accounting department. He wondered if the recently departed employee was the source of Lola's information about the Legacy Project, and if so, how the hell had she come by it?

The Legacy Project was a private matter between brothers. He'd not mentioned it to anyone, and he didn't have to ask, he knew Joshua hadn't, either. It irked him that others knew of its existence.

Alex shook his head in an effort to rid himself of the continuing sense of impending doom that wanted to settle on him. He'd been trying to grab a few moments alone with Joshua since they'd gotten to the office, but so far the day had been too jam-packed with one thing after another to do that. And sure as hell, if he went and sat down in his brother's office to have that chat now, someone would call, or walk in, or something.

"Coffee break," Alex said aloud as he pushed to his feet. He'd grab Josh and they'd head downstairs to the restaurant for some coffee and serious talk.

It would be natural to assume that if the honchos of the company were in a public coffee shop, anyone would feel free to approach them, but that generally didn't happen. In fact, they'd often joked the coffee shop seemed to be the one place where they could count on being left to their privacy.

Alex headed across the reception area—Stella was away from her desk, for once—and knocked, then opened his brother's door.

Josh looked up from a file he was reading. "We have to talk about this Legacy Project," he said.

Alex grinned. "My thoughts, exactly. But not here. If your morning has been anything like mine..." He let the sentence trail off.

"Yeah, everyone wants a piece of me today. Let's go downstairs. Besides, I need a cup of coffee." Joshua closed the file, leaving it on his desk, and then joined him.

Java Joe's wasn't owned by Benedict Oil and Minerals, and at this time of day—about a half hour before most employees in the area enjoyed their lunch hour—was not likely to be very busy.

Neither of them spoke until they'd gotten their coffee and sat down at a table in the back corner of the café.

"I think we should shelve the Legacy Project," Alex said.

"I was just thinking the same thing," Joshua said.

Alex leaned closer to his brother, lowered his voice. "The project made sense when we came up with it. Taking a logical, analytical approach to finding a wife seemed the thing to do because this choice, this decision, is the most important one we'll ever make. But…it just doesn't feel right, thinking about interviewing prospective brides when we're spending so much time with Penelope."

Joshua nodded. "I suffered a thousand guilty deaths Saturday night." Joshua paused to take a sip from his coffee. "I feel things for Penelope I've never felt for another woman. In fact, I think she's different than *any* other woman we've ever known."

"Yes! Are we in love with her? I mean, sure, it's different with her, and she's special. But is she The One?"

"That's what I've been trying to figure out! I don't know. How do you know? How does anyone know?" Joshua ran his hand through his hair, a sure sign of frustration. "Matt has said more than once that we don't have a clue when it comes to women. Thing is, he's right. We both know that. I get a lot of things in life. Relationships, on the other hand, especially romantic relationships, just confuse the hell out of me."

"Yeah. That's why I think we should table the project," Alex said. "Let's spend the next few weeks trying to figure out if we're, really, truly, in love with Penelope."

"And not just if we're in love with her." Joshua looked as serious as Alex had ever seen him. "We need to know if what we feel for her is strong enough to build a lifetime on."

"And if it is, we have to figure out how to make *her* fall in love with *us*," Alex said.

"It sounds like what we need is another plan." Joshua nodded his head once.

"Well, there's no time like the present." Alex reached into his shirt pocket and pulled out his BlackBerry. "Do we need to start with a mission statement this time?"

"Not this time," Joshua said. "Unless you want to make a title page. 'How to make Penelope fall in love with us.'"

"That's good. I'll do just that." Alex keyed it in, his fingers moving deftly over the tiny keyboard. "Okay, what do we put down for number one?"

* * * *

Penelope worked most of the morning, writing her initial report for the Lusty Town Trust. Even though she'd just been to the first of the sites she planned to tour, she wanted to show her employers—all several hundred of them—that she had a plan of action, and that her time, and therefore their money, would be well spent.

The head of the accounting department had called and asked if he could borrow Andrew for the next couple of days, to cover for an employee who'd suddenly quit. Since her admin had been willing to pinch-hit, she'd given him the nod. That made today even more perfect for writing her report.

Penelope looked up at the beautiful sunny day beckoning to her from just outside the window.

The two projects she'd handled before coming to work here in Houston had been for small nonprofit organizations. In each case she'd only been given a tiny desk crammed into a larger office shared by several different people. This office was huge, and eerily quiet when she was all alone in it.

It didn't take her more than a couple of hours to write her report. She'd been pleasantly surprised by what she'd found outside of Brady, Texas. The former coal mine was nearly undetectable. Deposits in McCulloch County weren't very deep, and some companies might have been tempted to rape the land, leaving black, gaping maws in the wake of their harvesting of the lignite.

She thought the term "strip-mining" very apt, as the process stripped the land of all dignity, in her opinion. She'd seen those kinds of sites in other parts of the country, but such was not the case on the land owned by the Benedicts.

The tract of land included a river. She and Andrew had drawn water and soil samples, of course. She'd documented oak, elm, and pecan trees along the river, coastal Bermuda grass on the flatlands, and mesquite trees along some of the ridges.

Not a single bit of barren emptiness existed on the site.

Penelope had even seen signs of animal habitation, including white-tailed deer and Rio Grande turkey. She'd have to wait to get the results of the samples, of course, before she could close the file on Brady. But she believed it was safe to say that when the critters moved back in, one could call the job of rehabbing successful.

Penelope really hoped that the rest of the sites she'd visit were as well rehabbed as this first one had been. Yes, that would mean very little creative work on her part. But it would also be a measure of the Benedicts' good stewardship of the land.

For the sites still under development, she'd ensure there was no wastewater contamination, no danger to endangered species, and she'd be doubly certain all minimum safety and environmental standards were not only met, but exceeded.

When she was finished with this assignment, Benedict Oil and Minerals could take its place as a leader in eco-friendly business practices.

Penelope shook her head. The pride that rippled through her didn't make any sense. She wasn't a part of the family, or even the company, for that matter.

Bad enough she felt possessive of the two men who'd so recently become her lovers. Feeling possessive of the family name and history was completely unacceptable.

Penelope stopped and set down her pen. Maybe those feelings weren't unacceptable. Maybe they were only premature.

Penelope tried to push the mind-whisper back into its compartment.

Neither of the men had said anything to her about their feelings. And while it was true they'd gone out of their way to be romantic Saturday night, and had even treated her to breakfast in bed Sunday morning, none of that meant anything. It didn't mean they were falling in love with her at all.

Maybe I should come up with a plan to make them fall in love with me.

"Penelope Primrose, that is the stupidest thought you've ever had." Her voice seemed to echo in the cavernous office.

A plan to make a couple of men fall in love with her? The nerd part of her brain was working overtime, no doubt about it. She put her hands over her ears. "Compartmentalize!" She needed to put those sexy men, and what they did to her, both physical and emotional, back into the compartment marked "personal," and focus on her job.

She read over her report once more then nodded. Concise, well-written, it would do. She printed off a copy. She'd just go over to Josh's office and give it to him. And if she happened to interrupt him, and if he happened to reach for her, well...

Penelope took a moment to save the file, and then e-mailed it to the Lusty Town Trust.

Printed pages in hand, she left her office.

"I don't know if either of the honchos are riding their desks at the moment," Stella said from her large reception console. "Most likely they've taken themselves off to Java Joe's, thinking I won't know where they are."

Penelope grinned. She felt a little sorry for Josh and Alex. They'd inherited their administrative assistant from their Uncle Carlson. Josh had told her there was something about having swatted them on their behinds when they'd been three that made it difficult for Stella to treat them as her bosses now. Any other executive she had ever met wouldn't have hesitated to send Stella Wyse to another department and pick an admin who would kowtow to their every whim.

Penelope knew *that* possibility had never even occurred to either of the brothers Benedict.

"Well, I'll just put this report on Josh's desk. I might leave him a note, too." And maybe, she thought, she'd go downstairs and join them for a cup of joe.

Stella was prevented from answering her by a ringing phone. Instead, she waved her hand, and answered the call.

Penelope walked across the central reception area, passed the comfy-looking chairs, dark side tables, and neat stacks of magazines. In the week or so that she'd been coming in to work, she'd seen people waiting from time to time, but was also aware they never had to wait long.

Josh's door was wide open. She still paused to make sure there was no one inside. She didn't want to interrupt unannounced just in case Stella had it wrong and Josh was inside.

She should have known better, of course. She thought the able older woman likely knew everything under the sun—including the fact that Penelope was having some sort of relationship with the "honchos" as she called them.

Her stomach rumbled as she crossed the carpeted office toward Josh's desk. Maybe she'd grab a sandwich to go with that coffee. Java Joe featured freshly made sandwiches and salads and soups, what she liked to think of as healthy eats. She'd already figured out that if she wanted a burger, fries, or traditional Texas barbecue, she needed to head on down the street to any of the many eateries catering to the business crowd in the downtown core.

Penelope placed her report beside a manila file folder that sat just left from center on the desk. As she turned to leave, the name on the folder caught her attention.

In a bold script, she read, The Legacy Project.

Neither brother had been very forthcoming about their precise plans to make Benedict Oil and Minerals a more eco-friendly company. She'd hoped they'd have opened up to her about their plans, because she had so many ideas on that front. Between wind and solar power, Penelope truly believed the country could say good-bye to using fossil fuels within the next two decades, if only businesses would put the full weight of their resources to the problem.

She hesitated for only a moment. The file wasn't marked top secret, or even confidential. She had no intention of sharing any information she'd come into with any competitors. She just—well, she was just nosy.

She really wanted to see how far along their planning had come, and which direction they were moving in.

Decision made, Penelope rounded the desk, sat in Josh's chair, opened the folder, and began to read.

Chapter 17

"There's Penelope now. Uh-oh, she looks steamed," Alex said.

Josh looked over to where Alex had his gaze fixed. He couldn't say for certain that he'd ever seen that particular expression on Penelope's face before. She did look steamed.

"I don't think she's seen us. Has she?" he asked his brother.

"I just noticed her as she went up to the counter," Alex said. "So I don't think she knows we're here."

"I wonder what's happened to upset her?" Josh asked.

"I don't know. Wow, she must be thirsty," Alex said.

"Two large cups of grape punch, yeah, she must be. Or maybe she's expecting someone to join her and that's what's got her ticked," Josh said.

"Yeah, that must be it because she's getting two bowls of the Pasta Marinara special." Alex turned to give him a quick look. "I'll tell you one thing. We're going to have to do better at reading her expressions…you know, if she's The One."

Josh knew exactly what Alex meant. "I hear you. Like the way the dads always know when Mom needs some extra care and attention," he said.

"Or when she wants to be just left alone," Alex agreed.

His fathers had once explained to him that every woman had "tells," just like every poker player. The smart man learned his woman's tells and what they meant. Josh's gaze didn't stray from Penelope. He watched as she carried her tray containing the two large take-out cups and two medium Styrofoam bowls to the cashier. She hadn't even taken a moment to fit the cups with lids and straws. She hadn't bothered with dinner rolls, either, or cutlery.

Joshua believed there was no such thing as too much knowledge. He knew Penelope was detail-oriented. One look at that lovely table she'd set for them the other night had told him that. Now, he focused on what he could see of Penelope's face, cataloguing her exact expression. If he had to name the emotion running hot—their woman was nothing if not hot—through her at the moment, he didn't think the word anger quite fit. Not even fury, because there, right there, her chin quivered as if she was trying very hard not to cry.

"Looking at the pain on her face makes my stomach hurt," Alex said. "No one's pain, not even yours, has ever made my stomach hurt. I think that's a significant sign, don't you?"

"Yeah, I do, because I'm having the same reaction. Someone has hurt *her*, badly," Josh said. "If I get my hands on the bastard, he'll be one sorry son of a bitch."

"We'll toss a coin to see which one of us gets to beat on him first. Okay, she's paying for the food. Let's get her attention and—" Alex stopped speaking.

Penelope had picked up her tray, turned, and was headed straight for them.

Joshua met her gaze, and he got another bad feeling. He didn't like the way her eyes had gone all cold, as if she was trying hard not to let him see her thoughts.

Actually, she was doing a hell of a good job of that.

"Gentlemen."

She set the tray on the edge of their table. "I was concerned that the pasta would be too hot. So I bought the ice-cold grape punch, too."

Josh took his eyes off her for just a second, to exchange a quick, questioning look with Alex.

Utter shock held him immobile as warm, gooey pasta slithered down his face from the top of his head, the scent of tomato and oregano strong and appetizing, even under the circumstances.

The grape punch followed.

He looked at Alex, wearing a similar lunch, and felt the bottom drop out of his world.

Penelope leaned down toward them. "What was I, just the side piece? Good enough to fuck and keep the edge off while you looked for some paragon of a woman to marry? You dirty, rotten, sons of bitches."

Her voice trembled with her emotions, the British accent growing thicker with every word.

"We can explain!" Alex said.

"No, sweetheart, you've got it all—" Josh spoke at the same time his brother did, but Penelope was beyond listening.

"Shut up! Just shut up, the two of you! I read the damn file. You left it right out on your desk! I know all about not being good enough, you bastards. That's been the story of my life, but do you know what? You might believe I'm not good enough for you to marry. But I've just discovered, the two of you aren't good enough for me. And I was stupid, *stupid* to fall in love with you!"

Her voice broke, and when Josh focused on her eyes, he saw the tears gathering.

Before his brain could function to form another sentence, she turned and ran out of the café. Josh jumped to his feet, determined to chase after her.

Another lump of sodden pasta slithered off the top of his head to land with a wet plop on the table.

He turned to look at Alex, who'd also stood. If the situation wasn't so horrible, he'd laugh at the picture his brother made.

"Oh, shit, we've really fucked up this time," Alex said.

"Yeah." Joshua tried to get some of the food off himself. Joe, who'd stood back and watched the scene unfold, finally came over with a couple of handfuls of napkins.

Josh had to give the man credit for not laughing out loud. He and Alex cleaned themselves up as best as they could.

"I've got some spare clothes in my office," Alex said.

"Me, too." They both kept jogging pants and tees in their closets for the times when they needed to hit the exercise room here at the office.

Without saying another word, they headed for the elevators. Josh ignored the snickers of passersby and kept his gaze locked dead ahead. The elevator wasn't overly packed as they were heading up because most of their employees were heading down for lunch.

Finally, the doors opened on the executive floor. Stella sat at her desk. It had to be a cruel trick of fate, Joshua thought, that she would be a witness to his and his brother's humiliation.

She spared them only a slight glance. "I see Penelope found you."

Josh narrowed his eyes at the woman. "Not one more word." He'd had enough of people laughing behind his back. Fine, he was book smart and life stupid. The time had come to get life smart, and fast.

"I'll grab my clothes and come to your office," Alex said.

He nodded and sidestepped to look into Penelope's office—empty, of course. Then he headed to his own.

"Boy, howdy, what's that you're wearing there, almost brother-in-law?" Ryder Magee got to his feet and Josh wanted to swear.

"Looks like the grapes of wrath," Colt Evans deadpanned.

Stella likely would have told him Colt and Ryder were in his office, but he'd ordered her not to speak. Need overruled pride. Colt and Ryder had managed to win his prickly sister over. That made them experts in the man-woman-man tango. Right then he knew that he and Alex needed all the help they could get.

"We fucked up," Joshua said baldly.

"You think?" Colt asked.

"Oh, great, company." Alex came into the office and closed the door. "Now our humiliation is complete."

Josh shrugged. "We could use their advice."

"You could both use a *shower*," Colt said. "That's my first piece of advice."

"We'll have to make do with the sink in the bathroom, here. We don't have time to shower." Josh began to peel out of his clothes.

"We have to find Penelope and explain." Alex dropped his clothes where he stood.

"I'm thinking the two of you could maybe use a little relationship counseling?" Colt's expression had turned serious.

Josh guessed the man could sense how upset he and Alex were.

"Yeah." Josh nodded.

"Then why don't you lay it out for us as you get cleaned up?" Ryder said. "Tell us what's happened. We'll do the best we can to help you out."

"Good plan," Alex said.

Josh sighed, and began to lay his soul, as well as his body, completely bare.

* * * *

Kate Benedict reached for the teapot steeping on the stone hot plate on the dining room table in what the family called the Big House. Steam rose as she poured, the scent of the Darjeeling comfortable and familiar as it filled her cup.

In her attempts to help the newly abandoned Penelope adjust to life in the United States, her good friend Eloise had looked for small, familiar customs she could integrate into their daily life and had adopted the English habit of afternoon tea. Kate, who'd happened to be there when Penelope had first arrived and had visited often, liked the habit and had taken it up herself.

There was indeed something satisfying about taking time out in the early afternoon for a cup of hot tea, and perhaps a small snack. She found it a wonderful way to take stock of her day and review her evening plans.

Bernice came into the dining room, a plate of ginger snaps in her hand. The men had just been sent off to run errands that should keep them busy for the next half hour or so, ensuring the women wouldn't be interrupted by male reasoning when they needed that quality the least.

Timing, Kate had always maintained, was everything.

She poured a cup of tea for her daughter-in-law. The sound of tires driving then stopping on gravel, followed by the slam of a car door, reached them.

"She made alarmingly good time," Bernice said.

"Indeed. Thank God she got here safely," Kate said.

"You know her very well," Bernice said.

"I've had years to get to know and to love Penelope," Kate said. "I couldn't have a better prospective granddaughter-in-law if I chose her myself."

"Didn't you?" Bernice asked.

Kate smiled, because there was no censure in the question. "No. I just opened a window. The rest was—and is—up to them."

The expected knock on the door echoed through the house. Bernice took one more long sip of her tea then set the cup down.

"I'll just go answer the door, now."

"Yes, please," Kate said.

Kate picked up her own cup, and listened shamelessly.

"Good afternoon, Mrs. Benedict. Is Grandma Kate here?"

Because she knew her so well, Kate heard the quaver in Penelope's voice. She smiled as she imagined the look on her grandsons' faces when she'd hit them with whatever it was she'd dumped on them. Stella had said she'd smelled spaghetti sauce and grape juice. Kate could only hope Josh and Alex proved to be their usual fast-learning selves.

"Penelope! My, this is a lovely surprise. Yes, Kate is here. We're just sitting down to tea. Please, won't you come in and join us?"

"I'm afraid I won't be here long enough—"

"Of course you will, sweetheart. I'm sure whatever it is you need to speak to Kate about will wait long enough for a good cup of tea. We're having Darjeeling today."

Kate tried not to laugh at the way her daughter-in-law bulldozed the young woman, even if it was very well done.

"Kate, look who's come to tea," Bernice said.

"Penelope! How wonderful to see you, sweetheart. Please, sit right down here, next to me."

"I'll just go get us another cup," Bernice said.

"Thank you, Bernice," Kate said.

"I'm afraid you may not think it's wonderful to see me when I tell you that I've come here to give you my resignation. I quit!"

Kate could see that Penelope really was upset, and that hurt her. She truly loved the girl as if she was her own kin. But sometimes, Kate knew, a little pain was necessary in life, in order for one to grow.

"I'm afraid that resigning is just not possible, dear," Kate said. "Do sit down. You need a good cup of tea. You know how everything looks better after afternoon tea."

Penelope looked a little bewildered as she lowered herself to a chair. "Not possible? Surely I can resign if I want to. This is a free country, after all."

"It is indeed, and yes, you could quit, if you were able and willing to pay the twenty-million-dollar breach of contract fine."

Penelope blinked. "*Twenty-million-dollar breach of contract fine?*"

"Mm, yes. It's all right there in your contract, in black and white." Kate used her cup as a pointer, but kept her voice even, as if she was discussing the weather. She'd included the clause in the fine print because, knowing her grandsons as she did, she'd been pretty certain that the course of true love would not run smooth with them. "That would be the contract you signed, and that was notarized, when you were hired by the Town Trust."

Bernice returned to the dining room carrying a cup and saucer. She set it down in front of Penelope, and took a moment to caress the young woman's hair. Kate poured her some tea and then passed her the cream.

"I can't keep working for you." Penelope looked near tears. "You don't understand."

"You'd be surprised what we understand," Kate said. "Men, even much-beloved grandsons, can be a real challenge sometimes."

Penelope opened her mouth, then closed it again. She looked from Kate, to Bernice, then back down at her tea. Adding cream to it, she stirred the beverage for several moments. "Challenge is too tame a word for those two," she said. "Try flaming, all-out pains in the ass!"

"My youngest sons *are* more of a pain in the ass than most. I'm not proud of that fact," Bernice said, "but I am aware of it. Ask Susan about them, and I'm sure you'll get an earful, too."

"Susan?" Penelope looked completely confused.

The front door opened. "Mom, Grandma? Am I in time for tea?"

Kate waited until her granddaughter came into the room. "Your timing, as always, darling, is perfect."

Penelope looked up at Susan, then back at Kate. She narrowed her eyes. "Why do I have the feeling I've been set up?"

"Not set up," Kate lied with a straight face. "Just anticipated. Stella called and alerted us you might be headed this way."

"We're probably not the ones you need right now," Bernice said. "Because we're older. But Susan and Kelsey are both very good listeners. You'll stay here tonight, of course. While you younger ones go have a good chin wag, I'll make up the guest room."

"Go on," Kate said. She laid her hand over Penelope's and gave it a gentle squeeze. "You're one of ours, sweetheart, and we take care of our own. It's the Benedict way."

Chapter 18

Alex tried to keep worry from morphing into stark terror.

They couldn't find Penelope.

"Mitchell says she took her car, so we know she's driving. But she didn't come here. And she hasn't returned to the office." He ran a hand through his hair—one of his brother's affectations—then looked at Josh. "Damn it, Josh, where could she be?"

Josh paced back and forth in the living room of the penthouse in front of the picture window that afforded a magnificent view of Houston.

"Okay, we need to have someone contact the hospitals. We can't report her as missing, not yet. She's only been gone four hours and thirty-seven minutes."

Colt came into the room. He handed a cup of coffee to Alex.

He didn't want the brew but had taken the cup automatically when Colt had handed it to him. The thought of putting anything in his stomach at the moment made him want to puke.

"You need to relax, man. Susan just called me. Penelope is in Lusty, safe and sound."

"Lusty? What the hell is she doing there?" Josh asked

"She went to give Grandma Kate her resignation," Colt said.

Ryder, who lounged on the sofa with his feet up on the ottoman, gave a low whistle. "You boys *really* pissed her off."

"We didn't mean to!" Alex sat down in one of the armchairs. Relief that his woman had been located, that she was safe, took all the starch out of his knees.

"We'll have that engraved on your tombstones," Colt said. "It's on the same level as 'I didn't know the gun was loaded.'"

Alex tilted his head and looked at his almost brother-in-law. "That was an odd thing to say."

Colt nodded, sat down, then looked over at Ryder. Alex couldn't read the look the two men exchanged, but something about Ryder's smirk put his brain on high alert.

"Now that your woman's been located, you two need to sit down and listen up."

Josh turned and met Alex's gaze. Without saying anything, he came and sat down on the arm of the chair Alex was in.

"All right," Josh said. "We're listening."

"Even though we've a month until our wedding, Ryder, Susie and I decided to begin working on starting our family," Colt said.

"Colt and I wanted the question of fatherhood to be completely in the hands of fate. To us, it really doesn't matter which one of us supplies the sperm," Ryder said.

"That's what the dads say," Alex said. "You don't have to worry. Josh and I have it all figured out, that—"

"You need to be quiet and listen," Colt said. "Because we felt that way, Susan came up with an idea. We're not completely sure if it will work, but it might work, so we decided to give it a try."

"Susan took the box of condoms that we keep in the bedside table at the ranch and used a needle to poke a couple of holes in several of them," Ryder said.

"She did that the day before the last Town Trust meeting," Colt said.

"The day before you met your Penelope," Ryder added.

"I'm not sure what the odds are of that working," Josh said. "I know that some studies conducted on the integrity of prophylactics state that…" His voice trailed off.

Alex felt everything inside him go perfectly still. He looked up at Josh, whose expression had gone completely blank.

"Holy hell, Josh," Alex said softly. He didn't need to cite scientific studies. He knew what Ryder and Colt had just said. Further, he had no doubt whatsoever what it meant for them.

"Oh, man," Josh said.

"You're usually faster than I am," Alex said.

"Yeah. It must be the moment, brother mine. I never before had to process the information that, in all likelihood, in just about eight months, we're going to be fathers."

"Well process this, genius. You need to go to Penelope and grovel. Big time," Colt said.

"On hands and knees," Ryder said.

Alex took in the not-quite-restrained smiles of his almost brothers-in-law. "I think you're enjoying this," he said.

"Maybe a little. Face it, you were pretty high-handed, hinting that our continued business association would depend on our coaxing Susan off of her ranch and into our beds," Ryder said.

"While at the same time trying to prove to your sister that she didn't know her own mind, or even have the right to make her own choices," Colt added.

"We just wanted to help," Josh said.

"Uh-huh."

Colt and Ryder said that together, and to Alex's ears, neither man sounded convinced.

Josh surged to his feet. "We're geeks, damn it! We both pulled a solid 4.33 grade point average and graduated at the top of our class. We can figure out the best way to finesse a business deal and can analyze any corporate situation we find ourselves in."

"We just don't understand women. Period. Whether they're the ones we're related to," Alex said, "or the one we love."

"Do you love Penelope Primrose?" Ryder asked.

"Completely," Josh said.

"With all our hearts," Alex agreed.

"Then keep that in the front of your thinking, and let's figure out how you're going to win her back," Colt said.

Alex met Josh's gaze, then nodded. They were both more than ready to listen.

* * * *

"Those stupid idiots," Susan said. "They're my brothers, and I love them, but I never realized they were *quite* that stupid."

Penelope didn't really want to agree with Susan. She sat with the young woman, and Kelsey Benedict, at a corner table in *Lusty Appetites*. The restaurant buzzed around them, as it was the start of the dinner hour. Yet Kelsey stayed with them, doing her part to provide moral support on top of the triple chocolate cake and chocolate fudge ice cream she'd already provided.

Finally, Penelope couldn't take it anymore. At first she'd been totally confused by the way both Grandma Kate and Bernice Benedict had "handled" her—and no doubt about it, she had been handled. But then her anger, and hurt, began to slowly ebb away. Her mind, that always-working brain of hers, began to think back and reorganize the data it had already processed.

The date on the top page of the file she'd read on Josh's desk was September first. More than a full month before she'd even met the brothers Benedict.

"They're not stupid," Penelope said. "Their minds just work on a different level."

"I'd expect you to defend them. After all, you're in love with them. I'm their sister, so I don't have to be quite so generous."

She hadn't said a word about being in love with Josh and Alex Benedict. Since meeting them, she'd tried to downplay the reality and depth of her emotions. She'd let herself acknowledge that she loved them, but then would try and convince herself that the feelings she had for them weren't the real thing. That they'd evolved as a result of the stupendous sex.

Penelope sighed. She guessed it was time she fully and finally faced the truth. She did love them, and wanted nothing more than to spend the rest of her life with them.

Their sister might think they weren't great husband material, but the truth was, they were the perfect husbands for her.

"So, how goes the baby campaign?" Kelsey asked.

Penelope was brought back to the conversation by the personal question. It took her a moment to understand it had been asked of Susan, and not her.

"Well," she leaned forward and shot Penelope a grin to let her know she was included in the private tête-à-tête, "I came up with the perfect plan." She looked at Penelope. "Colt and Ryder came to the decision that they didn't want to know which one of them fathered our first child."

"Why ever not?"

"Long story short, neither of them thinks himself good enough to be a father, but together, they've said, they'd make a good one. They had very rough childhoods."

"Men are strange," Penelope said. "They've surely evolved beyond childhood traumas." Penelope blinked, because the stray thought, that she was one to talk, flashed through her mind.

Kelsey nodded vigorously. "Yes! And they think we're the complicated ones!" She tilted her head toward Susan. "So what did you come up with? You realize that in a case of multiple partners, usually it's the first sperm to enter the womb on the day that fertilization occurs that impregnates."

"That's why this plan is so perfect," Susan said. "I took the box of condoms and poked holes in more than half of them, then mixed them all up in the box. The men use them, never knowing if theirs is one of the ones that will let those little swimmers go to the party."

"You poked holes in your condoms?" Penelope asked. Her heart thudded once. "Um, that's clever. When did you do that? Just recently?"

Susan waved her hand. "The ones in our bedside table in Houston I just got to the other day. But the ones here at the ranch were done first. When I first thought of the idea."

"You only thought of the idea after we had breakfast last month and I told you *we* were trying to get pregnant," Kelsey said, laughing. "You are so competitive."

"Not competitive. I just like company. What could be better than being pregnant at the same time as my best friend?"

Penelope sat back and placed her hand on her stomach. *Oh. My. God.* She cast her thoughts back over the last month. She usually was regular as clockwork and...

Five days late. Her period was five days late. Could she be pregnant? Her memory scanned articles she'd read in the last year on pregnancy and gestation. Were her breasts overly sensitive? True, that one time she'd nearly come when Josh had nipped and then suckled deeply. Had she noticed a bit of a bloated look in the mirror? Was she moody, emotional lately?

She nearly blushed. She supposed some might accuse her of being very emotional if they'd seen her dump pasta and fruit punch all over her baby's fathers.

Her baby's fathers.

"Penelope? Are you all right? You look kind of green," Susan said.

"I don't think all that chocolate is sitting well on my stomach." To her own ears, her voice sounded weak.

"She's getting greener by the moment," Kelsey said. "I think she's going to boot."

Both women jumped to their feet. "Come on. There's a bathroom in back that's private."

Penelope let Kelsey and Susan lead her to the washroom. She really didn't think she was going to be ill.

Until her stomach gave one giant roll. She made it to the toilet just in time.

* * * *

A few hours later Penelope found herself tucked into a queen-sized bed in the Benedict family home, wearing a borrowed nightgown, and with a cup of chamomile tea cooling on the side table.

The nausea that had gripped her so suddenly at the restaurant had passed the moment she'd rid herself of the chocolate overload. Her head had been reeling since. Not only could she not let go of the possibility that she was indeed pregnant, but she'd been treated to more fussing over than she'd ever experienced in her whole life.

She'd been restricted to broth and toast for dinner, which was just as well, because after that chocolate gorging—an act that had seemed like a good idea at the time—she didn't think she wanted to put one more thing in her stomach.

Could I really be pregnant?

Penelope found it comforting to lay her hand on her middle. She'd always wanted children, someday. They'd fallen under the category of "dream." One she could admit to herself now she never thought she'd be able to achieve. Having children meant finding someone to love her, and that she had firmly believed she'd never do.

How could she expect anyone to love her when her own mother hadn't?

A knock at the door pulled her from her musings.

"Come in."

The door opened to reveal Grandma Kate, done up in robe and slippers, her silver hair unbound and falling to her shoulders. She held something in her hand that looked like an old book.

"How are you feeling, sweetheart?" Kate sat on the bed beside her and felt her forehead.

"Better, thank you. I think the combination of chocolate and emotional distress did me in."

Kate smiled. "Chocolate is good for comfort food, in moderation." She looked around the bedroom. "This is the room that Adam Kendall and Warren Jessop would share when they stayed over. Warren would officially be in the room next door. He worried the servants would discover the truth, you see, so he always spent some time in that room, leaving his things there, making the bed look slept in."

"This is a happy room," Penelope said. "I feel very comfortable here."

"I thought you might like something to read before you fell asleep." She handed the leather-bound book to her.

Penelope saw that it had no title on the cover, or on the spine. When she opened it, she gasped, for the yellow pages held writing that looked strong and feminine.

"It's Sarah's journal," Kate said.

"Her journal?" To hold something so precious, the thoughts of a woman who had, in a way, been an inspiration to Penelope most of her life, was a very special thing.

"Indeed. She began to write it when her sons Charles and Samuel fell in love with, and married, the same woman—Madelyn Kennedy Benedict, my mother-in-law. Sarah realized her words and council on how to manage two husbands might be of some benefit to future generations of women. The men in the family don't get to read it. Only the women do."

In the family.

"But I'm not—"

"Shh." Kate leaned forward and placed a finger on Penelope's lips. "Just read. Then get a good night's sleep."

The matriarch stood, and then leaned over and kissed Penelope's forehead. She left quietly, closing the door behind her.

For a long moment, Penelope simply held the book, the sense of history and love she got from it an almost tangible force.

Lying in this bed in this home that had been the foundation of a dynasty, Penelope felt a sense of belonging fill her. She used the sleeve of her nightgown to wipe her eyes, neither surprised nor ashamed that at such a moment, she would cry. She'd waited all her life to find this sense of belonging, and here it was.

She took one bracing sip of her tea and set the cup gently down again.

Then she opened the book and began to read.

Chapter 19

Morning sun streamed through the window, falling on Penelope's face, whispering to her that it was time to get up. She blinked her eyes and knew one moment of disorientation. It was the first time in a week she'd awakened alone, and that disconcerted her.

Then everything came back to her in a rush, all that had happened the day before, so that, for just a moment, she felt completely overwhelmed.

She turned her head, and her gaze fell on Sarah Carmichael Benedict's journal.

"Did you know you were birthing a dynasty?" she asked softly. Some of the words she'd read the night before came back to her, their rhythm soothing, their reality somewhat shocking from a woman born before the end of the American Civil War.

It is true, and should be noted, that men, left to their own devices, generally muck things up. I want to make one thing, therefore, perfectly clear. It wasn't my dear husbands who took that first step to bring us together in love and intimacy. It was I.

I, who had been sold into marriage by my father to a man who didn't want me; I, who had been the target of paid assassins; I, who had fallen hopelessly in love with not one, but two handsome gunslingers. I did not know if we would survive to the end of our journey. But after all I had been through, I refused to die a virgin, not knowing a man's touch, or a man's love. Not knowing the touch and the love of the men who had captured my heart.

Penelope sat up in bed, the covers falling to her waist. She'd long ago felt a kinship for the young Chicago debutante who had been forced from all she knew into a strange and dangerous new frontier.

Now, after reading some of her journal, that sense of connection felt even stronger.

A knock sounded, and the door opened. Susan stuck her head in. "Good, you're awake. How are you feeling?"

"Much better, thanks."

Susan came all the way into the room carrying some clothes, which she set on the end of the bed. "We're almost the same size. I thought you'd like some clean clothes for the day. I also wanted to give you a heads-up. My men came home late last night with my very frantic brothers in tow. They're downstairs now. Mom told them to come for breakfast."

"I'm not ready to see them." Penelope's heart thudded painfully. She really wasn't ready to see them.

She'd overreacted yesterday, no question about it. That stupid plan of theirs was really just what she would have expected them to do if they thought it was time to find a wife. They were as anal as she was. Plus, it had been dated before she'd even met them.

Oh, God, she'd poured pasta and grape drink over their heads in the middle of a busy restaurant! She was worse than that Lola person, whose actions had taken her right out of the running—Alex's words, exactly!

So where did her even worse actions leave her?

"I know you don't feel ready to see them. But Grandma Kate says you have to come down and have breakfast. There'll be a lot of us there. You don't have to spend time with them alone if you don't want to, but you can't hide up here, either." Susan reached out and touched her shoulder gently. "It's not the Benedict way."

Penelope looked again at the closed journal resting on the bedside table. She couldn't imagine Sarah Carmichael Benedict being afraid to face up to anything.

"All right, I just need a shower, and to get dressed."

"Breakfast will be ready in about a half hour," Susan said. "Other than that, take your time."

Penelope just shook her head. She'd bet the gamine-faced daughter of the household had used that smile to get away with a multitude of sins.

Penelope sighed. She knew where the bathroom was, so she'd best take herself there and get ready to face whatever the day had in store for her next.

As the water rained down on her, her thoughts began to clear. Susan had said that Josh and Alex had been frantic. She doubted very much that they'd be frantic and follow her just to give her hell for humiliating them in public—or to tell her they were done with her.

She thought back on the time they'd spent together, on the way they'd fallen all over each other so damn fast. They'd definitely skipped a few steps in the courtship ritual.

She used a fluffy towel to dry herself and made a resolution. She wouldn't fall into their bed so easily again. At least, not without some heartfelt words and commitments between them.

One memory from the day before stood out above all the rest. She'd told those too-charming-for-their-own-good lotharios that she'd fallen in love with them.

They didn't have to propose marriage to her, but they sure as hell had better man-up and share their feelings, too. At least they would if they ever wanted her in their bed again.

Stay strong, Penelope. You can do it.

She felt their eyes on her as soon as she came down the stairs. She wondered that they didn't rush over to her, so potent were the stares she felt on her. Doubts began to assail her. Susan had *said* they'd been frantic, but maybe she'd misread their feelings. Maybe they had been frantic because of the way she'd dumped on them—literally.

She snuck a glance and saw that they were sitting in two chairs in a corner of the parlor, and that Colt and Ryder bracketed them.

"There you are, Penelope." Grandma Kate came over to her and took both her hands in hers. "You're looking much better this morning. How are you feeling, sweetheart?"

"I'm feeling much better, thank you."

"Wonderful. I want you to meet someone." Kate drew her over to where Caleb was standing and chatting with two other men. One was Jonathan, Josh and Alex's other father. The third man, much younger, she hadn't met before, but he did look a little familiar.

"Henry, this is Penelope Primrose, my friend Eloise's granddaughter. Penelope, this is Henry Kendall, he's Adam and Morgan's brother. *Major* Kendall is a pilot with the air force, just returned from serving over in Afghanistan."

"How do you do?" She extended her hand politely, a little astonished when Henry took it in both of his.

"A heck of a lot better now that I've met you, thanks." And then he grinned.

Oh, she bet he was used to getting his way with a smile like that! And with that jet-black hair and those aqua eyes, she imagined he had women draping themselves all over him. She couldn't help but smile in response to that cheeky grin. Movement out of the corner of her eye showed both Josh and Alex scowling, and Colt and Ryder with a hand each on their arms. And then she realized Susan's fiancés were *restraining* her men.

Isn't that interesting?

"Breakfast is ready," Bernice announced. "And how wonderful it is to have such a big crowd for a change!"

Penelope gasped when she saw the dining table, much longer than it had been the night before. Just as they were sitting down, Henry's brothers Morgan and Adam, whom she had met, arrived. They must have been expected, as there were enough places set for all fourteen of them.

"How lovely," Kate said. "You two military men must sit on either side of me, and I can be the rose between two fly boys."

Also sitting down to breakfast, at the foot of the table, was an older man in a wheelchair. Penelope had met Michael Murphy briefly the night before. He was Colt and Ryder's adoptive father—a former cop and a friend of Caleb Benedict's—who had agreed to be a guest while he recuperated from an accident.

"Good Lord, Bernice, if you keep feeding me like this I'm going to gain thirty pounds while I'm here," Michael said.

"Now, Michael, you know you need to eat in order to mend." Bernice gave the man a big smile.

Both Colt and Ryder seemed to be trying not to laugh. "Murph, our future mother-in-law is a woman not to be thwarted," Colt said. "Best just eat up."

"You're a very smart man, Colt, to realize that," Caleb Benedict said.

"Thank you, sir."

Joshua and Alex were seated at the other side of the table and down from her, near the end, between Caleb, who was at the head of the table, and Henry. They were far enough away they couldn't touch her, but not too far to inhibit conversation. Susan sat on her right, and Adam on her left.

The table had been loaded down with dishes filled with flapjacks, sausage, bacon, eggs covered in what looked like salsa, eggs that were, thankfully, plain, as well as rolls both sweet and savory. The moment bottoms hit chairs, the food was passed around.

"Adam, would you please pour some orange juice for Penelope?" Josh asked. He looked at her and smiled. "Orange juice is rich in folic acid which is good for…um, just good for you."

"And she needs some milk, too," Alex said. "Vitamins A and D, are important for nur…um, nutrients."

"Orange juice and milk at the same meal?" Adam asked. He turned to look at Penelope and made a face as he asked, "Wouldn't that curdle?"

Penelope felt herself melting toward her men. They seemed determined to take care of her, and she was pretty certain she understood the reason why. But there was no sense in making things too easy for them. She'd already done that, and look where it had gotten her.

"I will have some juice, thank you," she said to Adam.

"Too bad there's no grape punch. I've heard you really like that," Ryder said.

"I've no particular preference," Penelope shot back. "I'm happy to use whatever's close at hand." She felt her face burn with embarrassment but was determined not to play the coward in front of such a large assembly of Benedicts and Kendalls.

"It's good to have you home again, Henry," Grandma Kate said. "I'm sure your mother is delighted to have all of her traveling men back in the roost."

"She was smiling a lot at dinner last night," Henry said. "Especially when I told her that when this tour is done, I'm not going to re-enlist." He looked up at the collective assembly. "Ten years in the line of fire is enough."

"More than enough," Bernice said.

"You've done your duty, no question there. Any idea what you'll do next?" Jonathan asked him.

"I've a few," Henry said. "Morgan and I've been thinking we might engage in a joint enterprise, or two."

Then the audacious man actually sent her a smile and winked at her.

Penelope felt her face burn and put her gaze down on her plate, but not before catching the scowls both Josh and Alex sent to the major.

"I always figured the two of you would go into business once you left the military," Grandma Kate said. "As kids, you were inseparable."

"And insufferable," Adam said.

"That's because you were the baby of the family," Morgan said.

"What about you, Penelope? Where do you sit in your familial hierarchy?" Henry asked her.

Penelope felt her back begin to stiffen as it usually did whenever anyone asked any personal questions. She forced herself to relax. "I'm an only," she said. "I came to America to live with my grandmother when I was ten." Then she grinned. "I always wanted to be part of a big family."

"And now you are." Josh and Alex said together.

For the first time that morning, she looked directly at the men. "I'm not at the moment, no," she said.

She wanted to claw the words back when their first reaction was to wince as if she'd hit them.

Josh looked down for a moment then met her gaze again. She saw a look there she'd never seen before, one that thrilled her, and not sexually, either. "We'll see," he said.

"Damn straight we will," Alex said.

Penelope let her gaze linger on them for just another moment, then she turned her attention back on her breakfast. Chatter resumed, and it was only at that moment she realized the entire table had gone silent during their exchange.

"Coffee, Penelope?" Bernice asked.

She hadn't even noticed the woman get up from the table to get the beverage. "No, thank you." Usually she loved a cup of coffee after a meal. She could smell it, and the aroma that usually soothed her this time instead rolled around in her stomach.

"If you'll excuse me? I'll be right back." She wasn't certain if she was going to be ill, or not, but she thought it prudent to remove herself to the powder room just in case.

Her reflection in the mirror there shocked her. She looked a bit wan. Since she'd put only minimal makeup on that morning, she splashed some water on her face, then pinched her cheeks to give herself a bit of color.

When she returned to the dining room, the men had, for the most part, taken themselves off. She pitched in, helping to clear the table. It seemed to her the Benedict women had the scrape-and-clean ritual down to a fine performance. There were few leftovers to be dealt with, and most of the dishes got put into the dishwasher.

Cleanup was over in a matter of moments. Feeling at odds, she decided to wander the house. She felt a sense of history, especially when she entered the library. Here there were more photographs on the walls. She saw one of Sarah Benedict with her husbands Caleb and Joshua, taken as they enjoyed their front porch—a porch that looked the same to this very day.

Sarah was looking at the camera, but the men were looking at her. The love she read in the men's faces nearly stole her breath.

It reminded her of the way Joshua and Alex had looked at her just minutes before.

"Penelope?" Susan stood at the open door. "Grandma Kate asked for you. Something's happened, but I don't know what."

Penelope hurried to where the elderly woman sat in a downstairs study. Caleb was with her, as were Henry, Josh, and Alex. Kate was sitting, talking on the phone, and she certainly didn't look happy.

"Now you listen here, Cletus Jones. Don't you go doing anything rash like contacting the news media. Give me and mine a chance to have a look at this situation. No, I'm not fluffing you off, you know me better than that. What am I going to do? I'll tell you what I'm going to do. I'm going to send the honchos of Benedict Oil and Minerals themselves, as well as an environmental scientist, right now, today. They'll have a look at what's happened there in that arroyo, and they will deal with it, you have my word. In two hours? How in the name of Hades am I going to get them clear up to your place in just two hours?"

Henry touched her shoulder.

Kate said, "Just a moment, Cletus," then held the receiver against her shoulder and gave Henry her attention.

"I can take them up in the helicopter," Henry said. "I need just thirty minutes to prep the bird, and we can be airborne."

"Thank you, Henry." She put the phone back to her ear. "Cletus, we're going to fly my grandsons and Ms. Primrose up to your place in a helicopter. They'll be there in just over an hour. And Cletus? I appreciate you calling me here, first. We'll clean up this mess. You have my word on it."

When she hung up, Josh and Alex spoke at the same time.

"Where? What arroyo?"

"What's happened?"

"You'll have to discover that for yourselves. Cletus wasn't very clear. We're talking up at the westernmost field. I don't even remember when we stopped oil production there. It's just outside of Rio Pecos."

"I know where it is," Henry said. "Spent a summer working on the remediation, myself."

"Excellent! Susie, you take Penelope to your place and get her some jeans and some sturdy shoes to wear, so she'll be more comfortable." She looked at Penelope. "Caleb will come by in a bit and take you to the helicopter."

Kate looked so worried, Penelope didn't even consider saying no. "All right. We'll take care of this, Grandma Kate."

The older woman nodded. "I've got my money on the three of you."

Chapter 20

Josh wanted to punch something—or some*one*.

As he pulled the Hummer H3 up to the hangar where the Town Trust serviced the copter and the jet, he thought that someone was standing right there, wearing a flight suit and looking cocky as hell.

He and Alex had bided their time during breakfast, certain they'd have the chance to get Penelope alone for five damn minutes to explain about the Legacy Project, and to beg her forgiveness, just as soon as the table had been cleared.

They'd planned to explain to her that they finally figured out they were deeply and totally in love with her.

Instead, they'd been manhandled by family and then swept along in the general chaos of an emergency, the nature of which he still didn't have a complete handle on.

"First chance we get," he said to Alex as he parked the car. "I don't care if we have to tell this Cletus to put a lid on it. First chance, we grab our woman and grovel."

"Bet your ass. I don't know about you, but I don't like being at odds with Penelope. It makes my stomach hurt. And I absolutely *hated* sleeping without her last night."

"Ditto."

It was a short walk to where Henry stood waiting beside the EC120 B Colibri, the new helicopter the Town Trust had purchased just last year. The copter's blades were whirring slowly, the bird obviously ready to fly.

"Get in back, buckle up," Henry told Alex. "Penelope can get in beside you. And you, hot shot," he said, pointing at Josh, "you get to ride up front with me."

"Figure you can fly that bird safely with a split lip, fly boy?" Josh asked him.

Henry laughed. "You didn't like me flirting with your girl, huh? I can fly it with a split lip just fine, if you figure you're strong enough and fast enough to give me one, geek-boy."

It was the kind of ragging back and forth they'd always done. Growing up amongst such a large family—everywhere he turned in Lusty, Texas there were cousins of one branch of the family or another—tended to make you take shots first and ask questions later.

Josh sighed. As much as a part of him would like nothing better than to try and take on Major Kendall and pound the living hell out of him, the truth was that the time had come to put boyhood habits aside.

Josh shook his head. Then he said, "No fancy tricks up there, today, Major. Penelope isn't used to flying, or the way we carry on between us. I don't want her any more upset than she has been."

Henry's laughing expression turned serious. "Don't worry. I'll be careful with your woman." Then he grinned again. "Besides, I have to be gentle with her. Kate likes her, and Kate scares the hell out of me."

"You're afraid of my grandmother more than you're afraid of me?" Josh asked.

"Bet your ass. Want to make something of it?"

Joshua didn't have time to respond, because just then his father, Caleb, drove up with Penelope.

"I've been trying to explain that I don't have any of my equipment," she said as she joined them.

"We'll see that you have all that you need," Caleb said. "Mother thinks the best thing we can do to fix this mess is to just get the three of you over there as quickly as possible. I happen to agree with her."

"The clock is ticking. Let's go." Henry opened the back door and ushered Alex and Penelope into the copter.

Josh jogged around to the other side and got into the front. He immediately turned to look in the backseat. Penelope didn't look her usually sunny, smiling self. "Are you all right, sweetheart?"

"I'm fine."

Her answer came quickly, but Josh wasn't convinced. One look at Alex and he knew his brother wasn't convinced, either. Alex set about securing her seat belt.

Henry climbed into the pilot's seat. "Buckle up. Headsets on. I've already conducted the pre-flight check. We're out of here."

Josh didn't even have his headset completely in place when Henry lifted off. He did hear Penelope's gasp. A quick check in back assured him Alex was watching over her.

"How long will it take us to get to the old Pecos site?"

"Well, since Cletus is the one who called, my instructions were to take you to him, which is shy of the site some. Take us about twenty minutes to get there.

Josh sat back, his eyes taking in the scenery while his mind began to rearrange all the information he had about the site, adding in everything that had happened today, beginning with his Grandmother's summoning of him and Alex into the study.

Josh only half paid attention as the scenery zipped past beneath him. He wondered how it was that things looked so different from several hundred feet in the air than they did flat on the ground.

The day had dawned bright and sunny, with intermittent white, fluffy clouds filling the sky.

He frowned when Henry banked the bird just slightly as he made a right turn. Joshua would have thought that they'd fly in a straight line to their destination, which would have been left—due west. He opened his mouth to say something then snapped it shut again.

Puzzle pieces began to fall into place, and Joshua sat up straighter, paid more attention to the ground flying past under him. He shot a sideways glance at the pilot.

Henry must have felt his scrutiny, because he returned his look, and smiled.

Well, son-of-a-bitch.

His agile mind reached back, looking for more puzzle pieces. Click, click, click. They began to fall into place, fast and furious.

Half of him wanted to celebrate, the other half wanted to protest, if only on principle.

"There's our destination, dead ahead," Henry said after several more minutes.

Joshua looked out the window and smiled.

"Hey, isn't that—"

"Cletus's place," Josh said, cutting his brother off. He cast him a look over his shoulder. Alex met his gaze, and then his eyes widened.

"Yeah," he echoed. "Cletus's place."

Henry set down the helicopter a bit of a distance from the cabin. He didn't shut the copter off. "Alex, help Ms. Primrose with her straps. She looks like she needs to set foot on solid ground again."

"I'm on it," Alex said.

Josh undid his seat belt, took off the headset, and then turned to look at Henry. The other man shook his head, then locked his gaze on the instrument panel directly in front of Josh. Then he met his gaze again, and raised one eyebrow.

Josh reached forward, felt the bottom of the panel. He nodded, and quickly peeled off the envelope his fingers had found there. He folded the envelope and put it in his pocket.

He hopped out of the craft, ducking down, circled the front of it, and joined his brother and his woman.

"…noisy as anything you think the man would have opened his door by now," Penelope was saying.

"Cletus is old."

"Cletus is hard of hearing."

Alex spoke at the same time he did. Then Josh said, "Come on, let's go knock on the door."

Only a couple of hundred feet separated them from the front porch of the cabin—although calling the building a "cabin" could be a bit misleading.

Penelope led the way, obviously feeling better now that she had both feet on solid ground. She lifted her hand and knocked.

The noise from the helicopter increased, and Josh turned with the others to watch Henry raise the bird off the ground and shoot off, really fast, toward the south.

* * * *

Penelope blinked as the helicopter rose off the ground and then flew away.

"Where's he going?" she asked.

"My guess would be, back to the hangar." Josh walked over to the corner of the porch and seemed to reach under the railing. Moments later he returned. He inserted a key into the lock and opened the door.

"What are you doing? Shouldn't we wait for Cletus?" Penelope thought Josh's presumption a bit rude.

"There is no Cletus," he said, and entered the cabin.

"What do you mean, there is no Cletus?" She followed him inside the building, then stopped and gasped. Beautiful hardwood floors, gleaming maple furniture, and a clean, fresh scent combined together to tell her this was no ordinary cabin in the woods—or in this case, open range.

"I mean, Grandmother pulled a fast one on us all."

"But what about the disaster? The mess we're supposed to fix?"

Alex smiled. "I'm pretty sure that *we're* the mess we're supposed to fix."

"And I think Grandmother intends for us to stay up here, alone, until we do," Josh said.

"Stay here, alone? You mean she had us dropped off here and then abandoned us? That she manipulated the entire situation? That there is no ecological disaster?"

Alex smiled. "That would be my guess, yes."

Penelope began to shake. How many times in a person's life did they tolerate having their lives clandestinely directed by another? When she'd been a child, she'd had no choice in the matter. She'd been manipulated as if she'd been not much more than a piece of luggage or furniture—moved out when she no longer "fit in."

She was no longer a child and would be damned if she'd let that happen again.

"Where's the phone? I'll let Grandma Kate know exactly what I think—"

"No phone," Alex said.

"And not much electricity, either," Josh said.

"Look," Alex stepped closer, "we're not too happy about being lied to and manipulated, either. But we're here, in the middle of nowhere, Texas. Would it hurt for us to get comfortable and to talk about things?"

Years of resentment rose up, a solid wall that wouldn't let reason, or emotion, penetrate.

"I don't like being lied to," she said.

"I know." Josh came over to her. He reached up as if to touch her, then pulled his hand back.

"Look, why don't you just sit down for a bit, make yourself comfortable," he said. "Alex and I will go out back, grab some wood, get a fire going in the fireplace. Or look around, if you like. This is a nice place."

"Yours?" she asked.

"The family's. It's where we come when we want to have a long ride on horseback, and a destination with no outside interference. It's really a very nice place to decompress."

Penelope wasn't certain what she'd do next, but she would appreciate some time alone to pace and think. "It is chilly in here. A fire would feel good."

Josh and Alex looked at each other, each with an expression somewhat akin to panic.

"Here." Josh peeled out of his jacket and draped it over her shoulders. "You sit tight, sweetheart and we'll be back inside before you know it with enough wood to get the fire going. I don't want you to be cold."

He bundled her up and set her down on a kitchen chair. Then the men went outside, and Penelope gave them just long enough to go around the house. She got to her feet and reached to lift Josh's jacket off of her. Oh, God, she could smell him on it, and having the leather wrapped around her was nearly as good as having him enfold her in his arms.

This will never do.

She needed to get her head straight, to deal with this…this manipulation. How dare Kate Benedict lie to her and presume to rearrange her life without so much as a by-your-leave?

Penelope shook her head. She couldn't believe that Kate would leave her stranded out in the middle of nowhere. There had to be more of a trick to it than that.

"Well, hell. I've got my cell phone." She wanted to kick herself for not thinking of that straight off. She pulled the device out of the small fanny pack she'd borrowed from Susan. Flipping it open, she looked at the display.

"No signal. Maybe if I move outside." She opened the door and stepped back out into the afternoon sunshine. It was cooler here than it had been in Lusty. How far did one travel if one spent twenty minutes in a helicopter? She shook her head and looked down at the cell phone's display. Still no signal.

She couldn't see any high ridges anywhere that would impede the cell phones operation. In fact, she thought they were *on* a ridge of some sort.

The ground wasn't too hard, and she thought there'd been rain in the last day or so. Had it rained in Lusty before she'd arrived?

Penelope shaded her eyes as she scanned the area. Twenty minutes by helicopter could put her some distance from civilization, but surely Grandma Kate wouldn't really have done that, would she?

Then Penelope closed her eyes and envisioned that flight, filtering out her nerves. They'd taken off, headed toward the north, then a gentle curve to the east, then south, and finally west.

That had to mean she wasn't very far from Lusty, at all. Likely only a few miles away, she'd bet.

All she had to do was walk south east, and she'd be back in town in no time at all. In fact, if she set off immediately, she'd bet she would make it in time for afternoon tea.

She imagined the look on Kate Benedict's face when she waltzed in and asked for a cuppa. "Strand me, will you? Rearrange my life. Treat me like a flaming chess piece." Penelope closed her mouth, the sound of her British accent echoing in her ears.

She hadn't felt this upset in years. Right at the moment, she couldn't see past the emotions roiling through her, the same emotions she'd felt that long-ago summer day when her mother had taken her to Heathrow airport and turned her over to the airline staff.

Penelope inhaled deeply. "Right. Let's get walking. I bet we have a cell phone signal in ten minutes, tops." She turned and gave one last glance at the lovely-looking cabin, then resolutely turned and, using the sun and time of day for reference, faced southeast.

Putting one foot in front of the other, she headed off to take back control of her life.

Chapter 21

Alex whipped his head left, then right, and then cursed.

Usually a stack of wood awaited just out back of the cabin, piled against the western wall. Not this time. Alex knew there'd be some in the shed. He'd helped fill the damn thing the last time he'd been up there.

Of course, the cabin wasn't in the middle of good bush land, which meant any wood for the fireplaces had to be purchased commercially and brought in. It was, he thought, one of the few extravagances his family indulged in.

Josh touched his arm just as he took a step toward the shed. "This was taped under the instrument panel in the copter," he said, holding an envelope up.

"Read it," Alex urged.

He'd been a little slow on the uptake today. It hadn't been until Henry was setting the helicopter down by the cabin that he realized where they were and that they'd been set up.

Here he'd been worried when he'd arrived at the Big House that morning that Grandma Kate would blister their ears for taking advantage of Penelope, and all along, apparently, she'd been hoping that they would. Grandma Kate had played matchmaker with them all!

He'd be mad as hell about that if he didn't love Penelope so damn much.

Josh opened the envelope and pulled out a single sheet of paper. He looked at it then gave one surprised bark of laughter.

"Well?"

Josh smiled up at his brother. "It says, 'I've gone to considerable trouble to engineer this second chance for the two of you with Penelope, when I'd had such a good plan for your first chance with her in the first place. For heaven's sake, boys, don't blow it.' It's signed, 'Love, Grandma.'"

"I've begun to think that this so-called ecological emergency wasn't the only thing she's engineered for us," Alex said.

"Me, too. I've been putting several things together in my head in the last hour." Josh laughed. "And here I thought we'd escaped Kate's scrutiny when she didn't ask us if we were seeing anyone or poke around in our private lives at the restaurant the day she came home."

"I think we both seriously underestimated her," Alex said.

"An understatement if ever I heard one," Josh agreed.

"Let's go get a couple of armloads of wood and get back to Penelope."

"She didn't like the flight," Josh said. "We'll have to make other arrangements to get back home. I don't think she should fly again, under the circumstances."

"That's what I thought, too," Alex agreed. "When we decide we're ready, we'll use the shortwave in the master bedroom's armoire and ask Grandma to send someone with a Jeep."

It only took a short time to trek to the shed. The building was locked, of course. Alex fished out the key from the secret compartment built into the window ledge. Inside, the firewood was stacked high and deep and dry, just as he'd left it. Alex loaded up on logs, and snagged a bundle of kindling, too. Josh also grabbed a good armful of wood. The cabin would be cool at night and in the morning this time of year. It was a little chilly now from having been closed up for the last few weeks.

As Alex headed back toward the house, his gaze sought out the propane tank, just visible at the other side of the house. It took considerable effort and expense to fill the thing, which the family used only for heating water. The small gas generator they'd installed provided just enough electricity to operate the water pump and the fridge. The generator chugged away, and the propane hissed from the tank into the house.

"Must have sent the men from the ranch yesterday to get things going," Alex said. "I wonder how long Kate expects us to stay up here?"

His brother just shook his head. "I'm glad Grandmother is as detail oriented as we are. It means there's likely food in the fridge, too. And I think she expects to stay here until we straighten things out with Penelope."

"I hope it doesn't take long to do that," Alex said. "It's been hours since we've held her or kissed her, and seriously, I think I'm going into Penelope withdrawal."

Josh chuckled. "You're not the only one, brother. Come on, let's go inside and grovel at the feet of our woman."

They opened the door and carried the wood into the living room, dumping it into the wood box beside the fireplace. Alex set the bag of kindling on the hearth. It didn't bother him that Penelope wasn't in the kitchen where they'd left her. She'd likely gone exploring. Still, he was anxious to start groveling. The sooner she forgave them, the sooner they could have make-up sex.

"Penelope?" He listened, but she didn't answer him. He glanced over at Josh. His brother looked as curious and concerned as he felt. Alex headed for the downstairs bathroom, worried that the nausea he knew she'd suffered during the short flight had come back with a vengeance.

The bathroom was empty.

"Penelope?" Josh's call told him she hadn't found her way to the upstairs bathroom, either.

"Penelope, where are you?" Alex began to go through the downstairs rooms even as he could hear Josh doing the same thing upstairs.

Josh came down the steps two at a time. "She's not up there."

"She's not in the *house*." Alex headed for the front door, not even bothering to close it behind him when he ran outside. He cupped his hands on either side of his mouth as he called Penelope's name. Then he listened, waiting.

There was no response.

"Damn it, where could she be? She couldn't have gone far. We only left her alone for a few minutes," Joshua said.

"Actually it was closer to twenty minutes," Alex said. "And at least another five while we searched the house."

"Shit."

Alex reached out and stopped his brother before he could begin pacing. "Let's think. She wasn't very happy about being 'stranded' here. So what would she do?"

"She'd leave." Josh looked at him. "I think Grandmother may have underestimated *her*."

Alex nodded. "That little bit she threw at us in the restaurant, about not being good enough? It got me thinking. She acted very matter-of-fact when she told us about being sent to live with her granny—about her mother not wanting her."

"But it's still a raw and gaping wound for her," Joshua said. "I picked that up, too."

"Take that and the dousing she gave us when she read the file on the Legacy Project, I think she'd react first and think later." When Alex and Josh put their minds to the subject of Penelope, Alex realized they understood her probably better than she thought they did.

"And she's very smart," Josh said.

"So she would have figured out that to get back to Lusty, she'd need to head southeast," Alex said.

"But not smart enough to realize how far it actually is, or all the dangers she could be walking into."

Alex nodded. He and Josh were usually on the same page when it came to important things. "You're thinking of the arroyo."

"The arroyo, the coyotes, the bears, the jaguars…" Josh said. "It rained last night, over this entire area. I don't know if it was enough to cause a flash flood, but still, it's a worry."

"Okay, new plan," Alex said. He scanned the ground, walking slowly toward the southeast as he did. About a hundred yards from the house, he saw a footprint in the slightly damp earth. "She *is* heading southeast."

"New plan?" Josh asked.

"First, we'll go back inside and grab a couple of rifles. Then we go find her. Then we give her hell for scaring the shit out of us this way. *Then* we grovel."

"Good plan. Let's move."

"Moving," Alex said.

* * * *

Penelope stopped walking and opened her cell phone. She couldn't believe it. There was still no signal. A quick check of her watch told her she'd been walking nearly forty minutes. An even quicker check of the sky told her what she'd really hoped not to confirm. The clouds that had moved in about twenty minutes ago were still there, more solid than ever, and she could no longer judge her direction by where the sun was sitting.

The athletic shoes she'd borrowed from Susan were a pretty good fit, but they weren't her shoes, and her feet were getting a little sore wearing them.

Her grandmother used to scold her that her temper would one day get her into deep trouble. She didn't want to think that she'd made a huge mistake storming away from the cabin the way she had. Yet the idea niggled.

Penelope pushed the thought aside. This was the new millennium, for goodness sake. It wasn't as if she was stranded, lost, in the Wild

West of two centuries past. Surely if she kept walking, sooner or later she'd come upon a road. Or a ranch. Or *something*.

A sound broke the late-afternoon stillness, a high-pitched, funny kind of a sound that could have been a dog in distress but that sent shivers down her spine.

Penelope scanned the area. She'd come down a long gradual hill when she'd left the cabin, but in the last fifteen minutes the ground had leveled out some. And looking around, she could see slow, gradual rises of land in two different directions.

She felt reasonably certain she hadn't gotten turned around since the sun deserted her.

Just ahead and to the right, a large boulder poked out of the ground. It looked like as good a place as any to sit and let her feet rest.

Would Josh and Alex have discovered her missing by now? More to the point, would they come after her?

She really should have just stayed put. When she'd discovered there was no ecological accident, her emotions had taken over. She'd been so ticked off with the idea that Kate had deceived her, manipulated her so that she'd be left alone with Alex and Josh. That she'd manipulated her just like her mother had done oh, so many years before.

But had she, really?

Penelope's inner voice was whispering to her that she'd missed something along the way. She sat for a long moment, casting her thoughts back over everything that had happened since Kate had contacted her back in New York, asking her to come to Texas. She reviewed everything the woman had told her, and everything that had happened since.

"Well for goodness sake!" There was no doubt in her mind whatsoever that she'd been brought to Texas, offered a plum contract for one reason, and one reason only—and it *wasn't* because Kate

Benedict wanted to ensure the ecological integrity of Benedict Oil and Minerals.

She'd been brought here specifically to meet Joshua and Alex Benedict.

She felt as if she nearly had it, her own personal epiphany. *Now why would that good woman want me to meet her grandsons?* And why, when it seemed as if she was ready to bolt, had Kate arranged this deception?

Then everything fell into place for her as if a great fog had lifted, and Penelope had her answers.

Kate's manipulation, if it could be called that, was nothing at all like what her mother had done. Her mother had sent her away because a ten-year-old daughter was in the way of her desire to begin a new life with a new man. Her mother's actions had been selfish and self-serving in the extreme.

What Kate had done was to arrange for Penelope to come to Texas to meet her grandsons. And that's all she'd done—arranged things so they could meet. Not out of selfishness, but out of love.

Grandma Kate once told her that nothing made her more content than when those she loved were happy.

She'd always known Kate had loved her, nearly as much as her own grandmother did. Penelope had felt as if she'd been left alone in the world when Eloise Wright passed away, but she hadn't been, really, because Kate had been there.

She wasn't alone at all.

The animal sound came again, sounding a whole lot closer and a lot more eerie. A flash of movement to her left caught her attention, and she tilted her head, just a little, to see what had moved.

Oh, my God, I'm really not alone out here anymore, either.

A few hundred feet away from her stood the scruffiest looking dog she'd ever seen. Not very big, its ears stood straight up, similar to a German shepherd's. His body, scruffy fur that likely had never seen a brush, looked a dull gray with flecks of black. But his skinny legs had an almost orangey-brown color to them. His tail, long and at the moment hanging straight down, seemed full, lush, and carried a black tip.

"Nice doggie." Her voice came out a little more ragged than she would have liked. The animal didn't look overly friendly. Then he opened his mouth, gave a couple of yips, and then a particularly long, loud howl. He took two steps closer. Then he looked to her left.

Not a doggie.

"Sweetheart, don't move."

Josh's voice washed over her, and the relief that rushed through her nearly made her faint.

She saw them then, him and Alex, out of the corner of her eye. They each carried a rifle, and each raised those guns slowly, pointing them at the animal.

"Don't kill him!"

"Baby, he's not a doggie. He's a coyote," Alex said.

"I don't care. He has a right to live. Please? Can't you just scare him off or something?"

The brothers didn't answer her, they just looked at each other.

"You're the better shot," Alex said. "Keep your gun trained on him. I'll shoot into the air."

"If he charges you, sweetheart, I'll kill him." Josh's tone sounded dead calm, and Penelope knew that was the best chance the coyote was going to get.

"Okay." She kept her fingers crossed the poor creature would escape to safety.

"Try not to jump," Alex said. Then he fired two rounds off into the distance.

The coyote started at the first shot, then turned and ran, fast and low, off toward the east with the second. In seconds, he was completely out of sight.

Penelope barely had time to exhale and let the fear slide off her. Josh and Alex both laid their guns down and covered the distance between them in seconds.

Josh hauled her off the rock and into his arms. She returned his embrace, holding tight, only letting go when she felt Alex put his hands on her and turn her into his arms.

He hugged her, kissed her hair, and then held her away from him. "Jesus Christ, woman, you could have gotten yourself killed. What were you thinking?"

Penelope opened her mouth to answer, then snapped it shut again when Josh grabbed her and turned her around to face him. "If you ever scare us like that again, I swear to God I'm going to turn you over my knee and paddle your ass!"

"We both will!" Alex said.

Penelope blinked slowly and looked from one scowling male face to the other. "I love you, too," she said.

"Do you?" Josh didn't give her a chance to answer. "We came up with the Legacy Project last month as a way to look for a wife. That's true. But once we met you, you were the only woman we focused on. And you're the only one we want."

"It just took us longer than it should have to realize we were all the way in love with you," Alex said.

"I'm sorry I dumped all over you. I never should have done that. I just—I saw that file, and I went a little crazy. It reminded me…it felt like—"

"Hush." Josh pulled her close and wrapped his arms around her. "We know what it felt like to you. You were right about one thing. We really aren't good enough for you."

"But we're keeping you anyway," Alex said.

Joshua kissed her, his lips firm, his tongue insistent as he tasted her, as he drank her. When he ended the kiss, she reached for Alex, and reveled in the taste, the touch and the flavor of him. *Forever.* It felt like forever since she'd been held by them, kissed by them.

"Let's go back to the cabin," Josh said.

"We need you naked and under us," Alex said.

Penelope drew in a deep breath, then took one step back, one step away from the brothers Benedict. Josh and Alex looked at each other, then her, their expressions confused.

Penelope wanted nothing more than to go with them, be with them. Honesty compelled her to speak up. She didn't know what the next few moments would bring, but she couldn't keep silent.

"Wait. Before we go any further, there's something you really should know."

Chapter 22

Penelope blinked, because identical expressions of confusion and uncertainty turned soft and warm and so full of love, her throat tightened with tears.

"What do you want to tell us, sweetheart?" Josh asked.

"Um…" How did a woman tell her two lovers who'd practiced very safe sex that they were quite probably going to be fathers? Her hand went to her middle, to rest above the spot their baby might, at that very moment, be sleeping.

Two gazes followed the gesture. Two mouths curved up in smiles she could only call joyous.

"Do you think you are pregnant, sweetheart?" Alex asked. Then he frowned. "We hope so, but how do you feel about that?"

"I want your children." Penelope felt her face color. Well, that was rather graceless, wasn't it? These two hunks hadn't even said one word about a future, or the long term, and here she was…

"Damn good thing," Josh said as he hauled her into his arms.

He held her tight, and Penelope sighed as she laid her head on his shoulder.

"Because we want you to have our children," he said.

"Lots of them." Alex grinned. "We tend to have large families. It's the Benedict way."

"And, we're getting ahead of ourselves." Josh smoothed his hands up her back, then placed them on her arms. He eased her away from him, just a little.

Alex stepped closer, ran a hand down her back, then leaned in and kissed her forehead. "I love you, Penelope Primrose, with everything that's in me."

"I love you, Penelope, and I will for the rest of my life," Josh said. "You're the perfect woman for us. Will you marry us?"

"Please marry us, sweetheart," Alex said. "We can't do without you."

Penelope had never felt so safe and secure, and so loved. The heat of these two wonderful men surrounded her as their arms surrounded her, as their love enveloped her.

She would never feel alone again.

"Yes. I'll marry you."

Josh kissed her, his mouth seeming voracious to taste and to tease. He pulled her deep, and every care soared free so that all she wanted was more, and then still more, of him.

"My turn."

Alex turned her into his arms, and his lips and tongue proved just as eager and just as arousing. She tasted him, his unique flavor combining with the taste of his brother, the two of them the most addictive and pleasurable elixir in the world.

"Let's go back to the cabin, sweetheart," Josh said.

"Yeah, we need you. It's been more than twenty-four hours since we've had you!"

Penelope was well aware how long it had been since she'd felt their flesh against hers. Alex slipped his hand in hers, and Josh did the same. They stopped to pick up their rifles.

"Thank you for not killing that coyote." She was glad the wild creature had escaped.

"I would have," Joshua said then. "To keep you safe, I would have."

"I know."

The walk back to the cabin didn't seem as far or as hard with a lover on either side of her as her journey out had been. Before she knew it, the beautiful building came into sight.

"Um, that reminds me," she said softly. "I don't know how to tell you this, exactly, but...well, I think your grandmother has played her hand at matchmaking."

She looked at Josh, then Alex, waiting to see how that tidbit of information sat.

Both men smiled. "See how perfect you are for us? We both came to that very same conclusion just recently, too," Alex said.

"And you don't mind?" Once Penelope realized that Kate had orchestrated everything, she felt certain both Josh and Alex would be mad as hell.

"Funny thing about that," Josh said. "Alex and I had both watched Grandmother try her hand at matchmaking with a couple of our Kendall and Jessop cousins."

"And we agreed that if we ever got wind of her trying the same with us we'd be some pissed about it," Alex said with a smile on his face. Josh was smiling, too.

"But then we met you, and fell for you before either of us was even aware of it."

"So how could we mind? We're even willing to suffer grandmotherly gloating," Alex said.

Then Joshua laughed. "Of course, once word gets out of Grandma Kate's success, the rest of the family who're unwed will begin to shake in their boots."

Alex grinned. "She seemed to have her eye on Morgan and Henry," he said. "I feel it only fitting that we tell them that very thing."

Penelope shook her head. "Henry was only flirting with me to get the two of you riled up. Even *I* knew that."

"Still," Josh said.

"Exactly," Alex agreed.

Their smiles vanished, and each of them looked at her as if she was the most beautiful, most desirable woman in the world. Her heart turned over in her chest, and her nipples hardened. They got to her emotionally, physically—every way a woman could be touched by the men she loved, they touched her.

"Please." She knew she didn't have to elaborate.

"You're so damned beautiful," Alex whispered. He moved closer, slid one arm around her shoulders, then used a finger to tilt up her face. He placed a gentle, chaste kiss on her lips. "Our very own goddess, come to seduce and enthrall us."

"I'm hardly a goddess." Before these two beguiling brothers, no man had ever made her feel so feminine, or so powerful.

"You're *our* goddess," Joshua whispered. "And it will be our pleasure to worship you for the rest of our lives."

The time for talking was over. Joshua scooped her into his arms, and she threw hers around his neck, though she had no worries that he would drop her.

She clung to him to feel the closeness of his body, to inhale his potent male scent.

She'd barely taken notice of the beautiful house they'd called a cabin. Josh swept her up the stairs, and she paid only scant attention now.

He carried her into a bedroom and set her on her feet at the foot of the bed. Cupping her face, he placed a string of gentle kisses across her cheeks. Then he took one soft, slow sip of her lips.

Joshua stepped back, and Penelope blinked. She caught sight of the bed. It had to be at least as large as the one in their penthouse—and the one at Susan's ranch.

"The beds are always so huge."

Alex chuckled in her ear as he stood behind her, his arms slipping around her waist. His fingers began to open the buttons of her blouse. "That's the Benedict way. A couple of members of the family went into the custom furniture business, way back."

"I suppose they had a ready-made market," she said. She tilted her head back as Josh began to kiss the skin his brother uncovered on her.

"The company they formed is still in existence, and thriving. They're going to be getting another order soon. We want to build a house in Lusty." Josh straightened. His gaze met hers. "Is that all right with you?"

The words swirled in her head with a sense of wonder that these two compelling men actually wanted to marry her, spend the rest of their lives with her.

"Yes. I'd like that. I want our children raised there."

Josh's gaze shot to her middle, then up to meet his brother's. "We want to see."

They made very quick work of getting her out of her clothes. Josh slipped to his knees and placed a gentle kiss on her stomach.

"Not much to see yet. It's only been a little while."

"But you know, don't you?" Alex stroked her stomach from behind her, then turned her face to his.

Call it women's intuition, or call it a mother-sense. Penelope *knew* she was pregnant. "Yes," she said. "I know."

"As soon as we found out about the condoms, we knew, too," Alex said.

"We'll have to tell our almost brothers-in-law that as much as we don't have a clue about some things, we sure as hell do about others." Josh seemed pleased by the prospect.

"But not just now," Penelope said.

It felt so natural to stand naked between these men. The heat radiated off their bodies, warming her. The gentle touch of their hands on her skin aroused her. She wanted to be with them, to feel them surging into her.

"No," Joshua said. "Not just now."

He rose to his feet and stepped back. It didn't take him long to strip. Then he drew her into his arms. The press of his skin against hers heated her, excited her. She looked over her shoulder, pleased beyond words when Alex cast off the last of his clothing and came to her.

A hard male cock in front and back, the press of them, this was just the beginning and even more thrilling to her now than the first time. "Love me. I need to feel you inside me. Both of you."

"You'll have us, sweetheart. We do love you," Josh said.

"Just surrender, baby, and feel how much we love you," Alex said.

Penelope sighed as sweet, fleeting kisses and long, gentle caresses teased and aroused her. Joshua bent down and nuzzled her breasts, first one, then the other, with an erotic promise of pleasure to come. His tongue, sly, tasted her. Then his mouth opened and suckled one already turgid nipple. His draw on her, strong and steady, pulled the strings of her libido, sending shivers low in her belly and tingles across her clit.

A moan of pleasure escaped when Josh smoothed a hand down, across her stomach, to her slit. She knew he found her hot and wet. She couldn't help her body's response to these two virile lovers. Just the thought of feeling them, touching them, fucking them made her pussy rain.

Alex thrust his hips against her, and the sensation of his cock nestling in the crack of her ass made her shiver with need.

"More." She wanted more from them. She needed all from them.

Josh let her nipple go, a tiny wet plop that immediately made her crave another suckle, another intimate kiss.

He slipped to his knees and gave her the most intimate kiss of all.

"Yes!" The moment his lips and tongue began to caress her slit and clit, Penelope pushed her pussy closer to him. Wet and wild, hot and hungry, he tongued and teased her, shooting her arousal so high she cried out, certain she'd come in the next instant.

"You're so responsive to us." Josh's voice held a thread of wonder. He returned his mouth to her cunt, brushing his lips over already hot, swollen, and vibrating flesh. She whimpered, unashamed to let them know what they did to her.

"You melt me." Though words were difficult, she wanted to gift her men with them. "You touch me and I dissolve into a puddle of pleasure. Please, don't ever stop loving me." She thought she just might die if they ever stopped loving her.

"Never." Alex caressed her face, turning her head toward him. "Open your eyes, sweetheart. Look at me. *Believe* me. We'll never stop loving you. We'll never stop needing and wanting you. Swear to God."

"You're it for us," Joshua said. "You're our one and only." Sliding up her body, he picked her up and laid her on the bed.

She loved them for understanding her, for accepting her vulnerabilities and her weaknesses and being willing to reassure her.

"We want to do with you something we've done with no other." He moved to her side, making room for Alex to join them. He ran his hand down her body, and she shivered with delight from his touch.

"We've never been naked inside a woman," Alex said. "Not once in our entire lives. We need to be naked inside you."

"I've never felt a man naked inside of me, either." Penelope reached out, placed one hand on each of them, to caress and pet male chests. Then her hands slid lower and she fisted their cocks and stroked them once. "And I find that I very much want to feel you that way—naked, inside of me."

Alex rose above her. "You're ours," he said against her mouth. Then he kissed her, his tongue bold and scrumptious, sweeping her mouth as if he had to taste every bit of her *right now*.

She wound her arms around his neck, urging him down, needing him to lay on her, press her into the mattress. She wanted, needed, to feel his weight on her, to know he was real, here, and loving her.

He resisted the ploy easily. He broke the kiss and grinned at her. "You're hot for me."

"Yes. Yes. *Please.*"

"Shh." He bent down to give her one very soft kiss. "Like this, then." He laid on her, kissed her. She felt his arms go under her and gasped when he reversed their positions on the bed.

"Take me inside you, baby. This way, so we can be three, together."

She would take him, but first she covered him with kisses, slow, gentle butterfly kisses and deep, tongue-swirling ones. She lapped at him, sampling his flavor. Oh, how she wanted to take him into herself completely! Yes, she wanted them to be three, together—so together that they would truly become one flesh. She wanted it all.

She slithered down his body, his unique aroma calling to her, making her mouth water and her pussy drip. She used her mouth on him, and roamed lower still.

Alex groaned and thrust his hips.

She nuzzled his hot, hard cock, breathing him in, giving him timid little licks.

"God, woman, you're killing me."

Penelope smiled, the husky words thrilling her. She moved just a bit lower, then captured Alex's cock with her lips. Sucking him in, she took him deep. Up and down, she swirled her tongue along his shaft as she feasted. When he reached down, when he combed his fingers through her hair, she rejoiced knowing she pleasured him, that she could make him tremble with it.

"Enough. I don't want to come in your mouth. I want to come deep inside your cunt. Come here, Penelope. Take me."

Unable to deny him, she rose above him, raised her hips, and then slid down on his cock.

"So good." She closed her eyes for one moment as she absorbed the wonderful feeling of having Alex's cock inside her. Arching her back, she rode him, the sensations within her a beautiful rainbow of colors swirling and blending, and growing brighter.

"Look at how beautiful you are, giving yourself to us." Joshua leaned up and kissed her. "You're so hot when you're loving us. I can't wait any longer."

He got on his knees and moved behind her. She saw him reach to the bedside table, and her body began to tingle, because she knew what was coming and craved it so deeply.

Alex cupped her breasts for one moment, squeezing them gently, tugging her nipples. Then he eased her down onto his chest. She went, laying her head on him, raising her ass, riding one cock and teasingly begging for another.

The slick slide of Josh's fingers against her anus, spreading the lube, sent tendrils of excitement shooting through her. When he pressed against the tiny opening, when his fingers slipped inside her, she moaned and pushed against him. Then she rolled her hips so that she pressed down, taking more of Alex's cock into her cunt.

"Easy, sweetheart." Josh's hissed words told her how badly he wanted her and how hard he worked to restrain himself.

His cock became a warm press against her, tempting her. As he pushed forward, she moved back to receive him. Burning, stretching, the pressure grew to a fine, searing pain that made her heart pound and her arousal soar. Instinctively, she relaxed her hips and inhaled deeply, offering him everything.

Joshua's hands on her ass cheeks felt firm and possessive as he spread them just a bit more and then leaned into her just a little further.

"More, oh, please…" Penelope's plea ended on a sigh as she felt Josh's cock slide all the way into her.

"God, that feels so good," Josh said.

"Your pussy just got tighter," Alex said as he gave his hips a roll, seating his cock even deeper in her.

"Mm." Penelope couldn't talk. She could only breathe and revel in the presence of both of her lovers inside her, a part of her.

Josh's hand shook as he caressed her back. He bent over her and kissed her shoulder. "Are you all right?"

"Mm." More than all right, she felt something new and wondrous. Because they loved her, she felt complete.

Penelope clenched her inner muscles, caressing them both, relishing her feminine powers when both of these strong, vital men groaned in response.

"Easy, sweetheart," Josh said again.

"Don't want easy. Not now. Want…need…" Rather than finish with words, she began to rock her hips, up and out, down and in, slow, steady, deliberate, and over and over again.

"Penelope!" Joshua cried out then thrust into her, even as Alex held her waist and thrust up. Back and forth they rode her, hard, fast, deep, and oh, so fabulous!

Penelope shouted as she came, a flood of rapture so intense, so good, it seemed as if the entire earth shook.

* * * *

Later, as the afternoon light faded to evening shadows, Penelope lay on her back, snuggled down between the men she loved, the men who loved her.

"Woman, you're something," Josh praised.

Both of her men turned onto their sides and looked down at her. "No other woman has ever needed us like that," Alex said. "No other woman has ever given us everything the way you do."

"That's because no other woman has ever loved you the way I do."

She leaned up and kissed Josh, then turned her head and kissed Alex.

"Of course you know this means we really ought to thank Grandma Kate," Josh said.

Alex grinned. "If we do, our cousins will be in for it for sure."

"You mean because then she'll play matchmaker for them?" Penelope asked.

"Exactly. Though I don't think she'll need to go to the lengths she went to with us," Josh said.

"You know she had to have written those so-called threatening letters that weren't really threatening at all," Alex said.

"Yeah. I figured that out just this morning. As well as the fact that Stella probably told her about the Legacy Project in the first place, which was how Ms. Dell found out about it." Then he looked down at her. "You're awfully quiet. When did you figure out you'd been set up?"

Penelope sighed. "Last night she gave me Sarah's journal to read. She said that only the women of the family were permitted to read it. But I didn't understand that she meant that literally until we got here."

"No complaints?" Joshua asked.

"I've got the family I've always dreamed of having, more on the way, and a wonderful future of love under two honchos. I've got nothing to complain about."

Penelope sighed as she realized the truth of her own words. The three of them were headed for their very own happy-ever-after.

And she knew one more thing. They all three of them deserved nothing less.

Chapter 23

Penelope soaked up the warmth of the impromptu party, thrilled and humbled to find herself so instantly, and completely accepted into the family.

They'd returned just a few hours ago, via jeep, from the isolated "cabin" where she'd pledged herself to join this huge family. Penelope figured she'd hugged more people in the last half hour than she had in her entire life to date.

She'd truly never been happier.

Once more Kelsey Benedict had thrown open the doors of her eatery, and once more, Benedicts, Kendalls, and Jessops gathered to celebrate. Unlike the first occasion Penelope had partied here—her very first day in Lusty, Texas—this time she felt as if she truly belonged.

The door to *Lusty Appetites* opened, and the voices hushed. Grandma Kate stood just inside the entrance, her eyes sparkling, and her gaze roaming the assembled mass of family, clearly looking for someone.

Penelope didn't hesitate. She left the side of her future fathers-in-law and went straight to the woman who'd been at the heart of everything right from the very beginning.

It didn't surprise her that her fiancés quickly joined her.

"Grandma Kate." Penelope could say nothing more because her throat felt tight. She guessed she didn't need to. When Kate's arms opened, she went, burrowing into the surprisingly strong embrace. All the other hugs she'd received had been great. This one was the best of all.

"Now I'll really be your grandmother," Kate whispered.

"You always have been, in my heart."

Grandma Kate's grin was so huge, Penelope wondered she didn't drown in it. She stepped back and first Joshua, and then Alex, kissed their grandmother.

"Thank you, Grandma Kate," Joshua said.

"You're welcome," Kate replied.

Voices and revelry resumed, and before Penelope could blink, she was seated at a large round table.

Grandma Kate sat on her right, her fiancés on her left. Looking up she could see Susan with Colt and Ryder making their way over to join them. Steven and Matthew sat on either side of Kelsey at the next table, and it looked like they weren't going to let her out of their sight or out of that chair. Penelope grinned. No announcement had been made, but if she had to guess, she'd say the Benedict family was about to have more than one new arrival within the year.

Two of Kelsey's waitresses, Michelle and Ginny, saw to distributing the glasses of sweet tea and soda. Bernice Benedict had pitched in, laughing at something her husband Caleb said as she set down bowls of chips and salsa for the hungry. Tracy Jessop, Kelsey's sous-chef, came out of the kitchen bearing a tray filled will all sorts of delicious looking desserts.

Penelope brought her attention back to the one Benedict she'd known for so long. She'd reasoned, and she'd thought, and she'd come to the conclusion that she'd been brought here solely so that she would meet the two men who most resembled her dream lovers, the men she knew now had been destined to be her mates. For Kate to have done that, she must have been reasonably certain Penelope would fall for them. In her mind, there was only one way she would know that. She decided to ask, anyway.

"How did you know?" She wasn't surprised when she didn't have to elaborate.

Kate's smile softened. "I don't want you to think ill of Eloise."

"I couldn't. Not ever. Grandma Wright took me in without a second thought, and raised me as if it was the most natural thing in the world for her to do. I could never hate her." Penelope would never forget that gift of acceptance. Her grandmother's generosity really had saved her.

"You have to understand. She blamed herself for the way Chloe turned out." Kate said.

Penelope noticed Kate hadn't referred to the woman who'd borne her as her mother. "She shouldn't have. I find it hard to believe that Grandma was anything but a good mother to her. People make their own choices in this life. The only one to blame for Chloe's choices is Chloe."

"Yes, I agree. But when you're a mother," Kate stopped, and shook her head. "I should say, for *most* of us who become mothers, the sense of responsibility for all your children endure, and how they eventually turn out, runs very deep."

Penelope couldn't help but place a hand over her abdomen. "I think I can understand that."

"Eloise made it a habit to look through your room, and to read your diary, so she'd know all she could about what was going on in your life."

"Ah." Penelope had written about her dream lovers there, in her diary. A part of her felt ticked. Apparently, she'd had little privacy. The rest of her—the part of her filling with maternal instincts—could understand the action.

"She told me about what you'd written down, about your dreams. She was frantic, of course, given the way Chloe had behaved. I told Eloise that such fantasies for young women coming into their own were normal. I even suggested to her that all the stories I'd told you likely had been responsible for your dreams in the first place."

"But you recognized your grandsons in what I wrote."

"Well, let's just say I took advantage of the situation. I don't believe in any of that woo-woo mumbo-jumbo. I do, however, believe in timing and propinquity."

"Here you go, ladies, sweet tea."

Penelope sat back as Ginny Rose, one of Kelsey's waitresses, set some glasses on the table. Penelope passed the glasses around to her men, and her soon-to-be in-laws

"Where's that new grandson of mine?" Kate asked Ginny.

Penelope knew she meant Ginny's son, Benny. She'd met the child briefly on her last visit to the restaurant, and could say without hesitation the little imp had stolen her heart, too.

Ginny Rose blushed. "I thought Steven was going to pick him up from school and bring him here, but apparently he handed him over to Adam Kendall. Benny loves visiting the Sheriff's office."

Her tone suggested the idea was the strangest thing Ginny had ever heard.

"Don't you fret, sweetheart. All little boys go through a stage where they want to be lawmen," Kate said. "Your Benny's in excellent hands with Adam. A more gentle soul I've never known."

"Yes, ma'am. I'll bring over some nibbles for y'all."

Kate sighed. Penelope watched the older woman's gaze follow Ginny. "So much sorrow in one so young," she whispered.

Penelope had heard some of Ginny's story. She also knew from Kelsey that Ginny had been seeing a counsellor, working on her self esteem, and after nearly six months living in Lusty Texas was finally beginning to relax around almost everyone.

Penelope couldn't judge the woman. There was, she knew, a world of difference between actions taken selfishly, and those taken selflessly.

The door opened, and a group of loud, rowdy men entered. Penelope grinned when she recognized the Kendalls. Well, she recognized three out of the four of them, as well as their pint-sized sidekick.

In the midst of those big, strapping men, soaking up the male attention, little Benny Rose grinned from ear to ear.

Adam set him down, and he ran straight to his mother.

"Mom, guess what? Adam showed me how to fingerprint a perp!"

Ginny's eyes went wide, her gaze shooting straight to Adam.

Lusty's Sheriff met her gaze head-on without saying a word, and after just a moment, Ginny blushed, and looked down.

"I was the perp being fingerprinted," the man Penelope didn't recognize said. "So don't you worry there, Ginny Rose."

"That's their brother, Jake," Grandma Kate said to Penelope. "Jordan's been tied up in contract negotiations for his construction company these last few days, else he'd be here too." Then she smiled at Penelope. "Really, it won't take all that long to learn who everyone is."

Just then Henry and Morgan descended on her from opposite directions. "I can't believe you'd choose these two nerd-boys over me!" Henry's tone teased, and Penelope couldn't help but smile. He bent down and kissed her left cheek.

"What can I say? I did see them first," she replied.

"Ah, well, you know what they say," Morgan said. "Timing is everything."

"Hey, Grandma Kate, maybe you should see about finding a woman for these two fly boys, here," Joshua said, "since you did such an excellent job finding Penelope for Alex and me."

Penelope laughed when Morgan shot his brother, Henry, a disgusted look, which he followed up with a punch in the arm. "Now see what you've done? You and that glib tongue of yours are always getting us in trouble."

"Sounds like a good idea to me," Jake said from the next table, where he'd settled down beside Matthew. "Since the two of you will both be mustering out soon, you're going to need something to keep you busy. I think a wife is just the ticket."

"Thanks, but no thanks." Morgan stepped closer, leaned down, and planted a noisy kiss on Penelope's other cheek. "Congratulations. Or maybe I should offer my condolences, since you've chosen to take on these two geeks."

"I'm a geek, too, so it's all very good," she said.

Morgan stepped back and looked at Grandma Kate. "I mean it, Kate. You don't need to trouble yourself over Henry and me. We'll find a wife when the time comes."

"You say that as if the right woman is going to just fall right out of the sky," Kate said primly.

"Well now, since I'm a pilot, I happen to know the best things in life can come at you from out of the sky."

"Morgan Kendall, you're a cheeky pup."

Penelope wondered about the tone, and if the older woman's feelings had just been hurt.

But behind Kate's bifocals, Penelope saw the light of challenge in the older woman's eyes. She sat and watched as Kate looked at Morgan and Henry, and then Jake and Adam. She recognized a look of cool calculation when she saw one. Then her glance went to Ginny Rose, and Penelope wondered at the thoughts running through the elderly woman's mind. She would swear she could see the wheels turning.

"Hey, Grandma Kate, when are you taking off next?" Matthew asked. "What's it going to be? Another cruise? Or maybe an African safari?"

It seemed in that moment that all eyes turned to the family's matriarch.

"Oh, I'm staying around Lusty for a while, yet. I have a lot of work to do."

A sudden hush settled on the assembled revellers. Then, softly at first, the sound of laughter—rich, poignant and satisfied, rippled through the room. Those Kendalls, Benedicts, and Jessops not yet married, however, each wore expressions of varying degrees of shock and horror.

Penelope laughed and threw her arms around Grandma Kate. "Oh, Grandma Kate, I'm so glad you're staying. And I'm so glad you're my grandmother now, too," she said.

"So am I, sweetheart." Grandma Kate hugged her back. "So am I."

THE END

Also by Cara Covington

Ménage Everlasting: The Lost Collection: *Love Under Two Gunslingers*
Ménage Everlasting: The Lost Collection: *Love Under Two Lawmen*
Ménage Everlasting: The Lusty, Texas Collection: *Love Under Two Benedicts*
Ménage Everlasting: The Lusty, Texas Collection: *Love Under Two Wildcatters*

Also by Morgan Ashbury

BookStrand Mainstream: *A Little R & R*
Ménage Amour: *The Lady Makes Three*
Siren Classic: *Made for Each Other*
Siren Classic: A Siren Adult Fairy Tale: *Beau and the Lady Beast*
Siren Classic: *Lily in Bloom*
Siren Classic: Magic and Love 1: *The Prince and the Single Mom*
Siren Classic: Magic and Love 2: *The Princess and the Bodyguard*
Siren Classic: Magic and Love 3: *A Prince for Sophie*
Siren Classic: The Song of the Sirens 1: *The Seductress*
Siren Classic: The Song of the Sirens 2: *The Enchantress*
Siren Classic: Song of the Sirens 3: *The Beauty*
Ménage Amour: *Wanton Wager*
Ménage Amour: *Reckless Abandon*
Ménage Amour: *Cowboy Cravings*
Ménage Amour: Reckless and Brazen: *Brazen Seduction*
Ménage Amour: Shackled and Shameless, a Reckless Abandon Novel: *Shackled*

Available at
BOOKSTRAND.COM

Siren Publishing, Inc.
www.SirenPublishing.com